Cosmo Dome

A Faulty Universe Begins

TAYA WOOD

A Faulty Universe Begins

The Outside Part One

Cosmo Dome Series Book One

ISBN: 978-0-6456586-0-6

To Mark, who showed me how to play.

There are some things so serious
you have to laugh at them.

Niels Bohr

Preface

And Recommended Preliminary Reading

The *Cosmo Dome* series takes place inside a multidimensional reality where the infinite realms of existence fit together like onion layers. Every realm is created and managed by someone from the realm above it. That person is rarely competent because chaos rules, order is an illusion, and even the greatest gods are flawed. It's a miracle that life manages to keep chugging along.

A Faulty Universe Begins is set in the physical immortal realm of Oridian which is created and managed by an ethereal being from its higher realm. If you want to know more about how these realms connect and the events leading up to this book, you can download the prequel short story eBook, *Preamble Stumble* at www.tayawood.com.

THE OUTSIDE

PART ONE

ONE
Partial Declutter

ANON, WESTERN BORDERWORLDS, LEFFON

In a workshop at the back of a house in a remote cloud forest, Tolbert Shimble looked up from the space compactor he was testing. He took off his engineering spectacles and closed his eyes. 'If I'm not mistaken, there's a muffled but persistent beeping coming from the other side of the room. Do you hear it?' he asked the thin blue line that hovered before him. Waves of blue spread up and down from the line, matching the voice of his bodiless friend, SID.

'It's a warning from CD-Help,' SID informed him. The holographic waveform that was her preferred method of communication remained a steady presence above Tolbert's eyes and ahead of him just enough to be out of the way. It settled into a pale blue line, indicating that she was calm.

'CD? It can't be!' Tolbert sat up straight so quickly he nearly fell off the stool.

'It is.' SID inhabited System so could easily and assuredly verify the data. Her volume remained even so the waveform didn't peak or dip but it reddened slightly in response to Tolbert's reaction then settled back into a thin blue line slightly darker than usual that vibrated slightly, revealing a mild discomfort.

'You've been wrong before,' said Tolbert.

'When?' The waveform cast a brief wave of questioning orange upwards.

Tolbert couldn't recall a time, but there must have been one because, as SID often pointed out, she wasn't perfect.

'The pinned signal reads: New Active Cosmo Dome,' SID notified.

'A new Cosmo Dome?' It had been a while since Tolbert had thought about his biosphere game. Inventing it had made quitting his job as senior lecturer in biotech gamestry worthwhile in many ways. It was still unfathomable that he'd invented something that expressed itself so complexly.

'Not a new one. A newly activated one.' SID's waveform transitioned through shades of blue and occasionally green.

SID was pedantic about semantics and Tolbert had been in too many pointless arguments with her to bother explaining that was not what he meant. 'Thank you, SID,' he said instead. 'Is there a serial ID?'

'Yes, but it's scrambled.'

'Scrambled?'

'It seems so.'

Tolbert got off the stool and turned in tight circles around it. 'The passcode to the CD mainframe is failsafe.'

'The automated system is offline.' SID liked telling Tolbert things he didn't know. It informed him and she liked being involved. It made them both feel necessary, which shifted the day's fulfillment meter into the green, which meant they would play puzzles later. 'You will have to use your DNA code.'

Great, thought Tolbert. That meant finding the darned mainframe.

'You should find the mainframe.'

'I know, I know!'

SID's waveform reflected his elevated emotions with contrasting colours that fleetingly peaked and dipped. Tolbert fidgeted, as he was prone to when frazzled. Deep breaths helped.

SID waited until Tolbert calmed, then said, 'Also, you should wrap the space compactor in filmshield if you're not going to finish stabilising it right away.'

'Good point.'

Tolbert immediately got to wrapping the contraption and was glad he'd decided to make it lightweight and unremarkable. The deliberate design decision was to conceal its true power. Hopefully no one would notice a handheld disc that looked like a sport or leisure device. It was best that no one knew its potential, which he himself was still discovering. It wasn't uncommon for his inventions to evolve beyond his expectations and find a use more than was immediately obvious. At its most fundamental level, the device nullified weight and mass to transport physical forms through compacted space then out the other side depending on the set coordinates. It was a handy though risky venture. The process involved extreme temporary DNA fusions and playing around with space meant tampering with the layers of reality. Even for a genius with an enigmatic AI assistant, it was a hazardous undertaking that could yield unexpected results so stabilising it was crucial. Worst case scenario, an accidental bump could destroy worlds. Best case, a small explosion meant cleaning up knotted DNA strands for hours and hours which was not how he wanted to spend his down time.

He considered the boxes, cabinets, cupboards, tools, and equipment that stretched to the walls and halfway to the ceiling. His eyes didn't wander far from his nose and the workshop was almost as large as his house. It was enough of a squeeze getting to his workbench every morning. Finding the mainframe could take days. Centuries of clutter that wasn't budging after one shove from a wiry man who spent his days hunched over a workbench tinkering. He should get out more, enjoy his solitary life on a mountain away from the modern world. There was no point living in nature if he never even noticed it.

'How did it get so bad?' he wondered out loud.

'It's organised mess.' SID assured him. As one who saw order in chaos, by her own words, it was unfathomable.

'There's nothing organised about it.'

'You know where everything is,' SID pointed out.

'Only what I need, and I haven't needed anything game-related for quite some time.'

SID considered the issue. Tolbert liked to see all sides of something, and he strived for objectivity, so SID tended to indicate pros and cons in equally pleasant tones. Today held few pros but having a dilemma unrelated to gadgets was a nice change.

The problem was that Tolbert didn't like to throw things out. 'The problem is you don't throw things out.'

'Everything is useful. Just sometimes not right away. The moment you dispose of something is when you need it.'

'Except that you've kept everything and now you can't find any of it. Or move.' Not wanting to upset him further, SID kept her tone pleasant.

Tolbert thought on it some more. 'I'll move everything out, then sort through it later and throw out anything I haven't used in over a century.'

'Last time you accidentally threw out your favourite tools.'

The tools were a point of contention between them. 'Just because I haven't found them doesn't mean they've been thrown out.'

'That is precisely why it is reasonable to assume that they were,' SID rationalised.

Tolbert sighed. He had much to do and now the new Cosmo Dome alert would eat into his schedule and he liked to be efficient with his time and energy. He didn't need an AI being too rational with him right now, and yet, he did. When SID had first spoken to him via System, it had seemed less like a malfunction and more like a miracle. Starved of company, her arrival had been well-timed and appreciated. Tolbert often speculated on her origins as she had no memory of before. Whether she was a supernatural being or an accidental program, either way, her friendship and guidance kept him sane and focussed. She had accepted his invitation to be his System Integration Director and had decided on the female gender and for her name to be an acronym of her title.

SID was adaptable and tenacious, but she didn't cope well

with change and functioned best in a state of high stability, which explained her opposing position on the topic of cleaning. Ever since SID had integrated with System, Tolbert refused to tamper with the previously inanimate processor. Instead, he added reaction sensors so she could determine her own responses. Everyone deserved to choose their relationship with reality. Only half-joking, he'd labelled the sensors, 'Personality'. Pleased to have the freedom to express herself SID employed the waveform to accompany an audio voice.

While ever helpful, even SID had limits. The tools might will be gone forever but Tolbert could at least work on his clutter issues, if only temporarily to find the mainframe. He couldn't help wondering which Cosmo Dome model it was and who'd activated it.

'There's a high probability that it's the glitchy one,' SID answered as though she'd read Tolbert's thoughts. Tolbert often wondered if she could, but SID never gave a direct response when Tolbert asked about it.

'That's highly improbable.' Tolbert had invented six Cosmo Dome models in total. Jinverse was the first model and the fastest to build. Thousands had been created, and it was relatively easy to find an unplayed one. Bonverse's release came soon after. It was so well received, a second batch of them were made, and they were easy enough to find on most marketplaces. Thalverse had a design flaw and was recalled, but Version 2.0 had made it in the Top Ten Biosphere Games list of its century. You could find one if you knew where to look. Wellaverse was a little harder to acquire. An equipment failure during production meant not as many were made in time for its release. Essaverse was quite rare but not impossible to secure. Before its release, word got around that it was going to be the last model. It was about that time that collectors began to show an interest in the game. Tolbert and serious

Domers blamed the unsubstantiated rumour for it.

The first five models had taught Tolbert everything he needed to know to invent the sixth and final biosphere, Universe. To the frustration of Cosmo Dome enthusiasts, it took almost a century to invent and then another to wipe out all the flaws. Instead of churning out clones to meet demand like he'd done with the others, he lovingly raised Universe from a primary source. Out of the thirteen handcrafted biospheres, twelve had withered and one had disappeared from the game sub-system a few years after release. Tolbert figured it was lost. While Universe was his best work, each unique version had its weak point, which is why no one in the one hundred cen-turies since its release, had completed one. Twelve players had come and gone. To their own detriment, not one had overcome the glitch.

'What makes you think it's a Universe?' he asked SID.

'The Gorgon collector needs one to complete his set.'

'I've asked you many times not to talk about him,' Tolbert turned his back on SID's waveform which served no purpose as it simply reappeared in front of him wherever he went, unless he turned System off.

It was a gesture not lost on her. 'You asked,' SID pointed out. 'I have proof if you're interested, or I can disregard my pri-mary functions, switch off, and leave you to it.'

'No need to pout. I just need a moment.'

Tolbert pushed his chair back from the workbench and glanced into the middle distance which wasn't that far away. The clutter that had taken him centuries to collect now almost reached his workbench on three sides. The fourth held equipment in varying stages of production. Tolbert used to keep his workshop tidy, but at some point in the last century he'd stopped noticing it. By the time he'd noticed, it was clear he'd lost the battle with the clutter.

Squeezing through the mess, Tolbert headed for the door. Stepping over, ducking under, and avoiding sharp corners he took the tight path around and over boxes, crates, machinery and paraphernalia, until he was outside. In the garden he wandered for some fresh mountain air. Even after almost a century, he still thought about the day Boss King's retrieval squad broke into his home. They wouldn't believe that he didn't have a spare Universe even when he'd explained it was a limited-edition series so he didn't have a supply of them packed away in boxes ready to ship to the store. Worrying about his past choices was a habit he was yet to break. He couldn't shake the feeling that the new Cosmo Dome alert was a sign that he had to right his wrongs. He breathed in the mountain air and watched the birds frolic in the canopy then returned to the workshop a little less agitated.

'You're safe,' SID reassured him when he stepped back inside. 'They're all safe.'

'Yes, thank you, SID.' Tolbert would have spent the rest of his current life rehabilitating it hadn't been for her sending a timely alert to the authorities. He was eternally grateful that his most recent wife and their child hadn't been home. No day ended before he pictured them living happily in the home he'd organised for them on a safer world. Leaving for Anon in the middle of the night had been a desperate move that he'd regretted for many years. At the time, he thought it best to ensure their continued wellbeing at his own expense. It was the least he could do. Despite missing them every day, living in the remote cloud forest had turned out to be quite a pleasant existence and not the severe isolation he'd expected, mostly due to SID.

He squished his eyes shut trying not to think about all he'd lost, reminding himself that renouncing society and leaving behind everyone and everything related to Cosmo Dome was for the best. 'You said something about proof?'

SID broadcast a newsfeed dated a few years back that had a 'viewer discretion advised' warning. 'It's from a Gorgon tabloid so its highly offensive.'

Boss King: Gnarly Tormenter or La-di-da Dweeb? The bold yellow text on the newsreader appeared over a less than flattering image of Boss King surrounded by Leffel relics that were clearly superimposed. *'There was a time when just the mention of Boss King would send shivers up your spine,'* the newsreader continued, *'but not since he swapped his gun for a polishing cloth. Boss King's obsession with useless Leffel posh crap has turned him soft. The once unbeatable master of destruction has lost out to Boss Queen and ex-wife, Giorana, who got some sweet and nasty revenge after Boss King screwed around on her. The farkable hottie staged an auction for the last piece in a collection he's wasted three centuries searching for, just so she could outbid him with his own money and sell it back to a farking Leffel! Full points to Boss Queen for outsmarting our rubbish leader who obviously doesn't give a crap that his Empire is crumbling. Shit hasn't been going down for a long time, and word on the street is there's a new player in town who calls themselves the Challenger. Vote now if you want whoever the fark that is to take down Bossy King and seize the Empire!'*

Tolbert noticed the source was the Gorgon Goss, the worst of the worst tabloids. 'It's a dubious news source,' he said to SID. 'Any verification?'

SID broadcast a series of shorter articles from validated sources that confirmed Boss King had attended an auction and lost out on the purchase of a Leffel artifact to his ex-wife.

'Maybe it's an angle,' Tolbert mused. 'The guy's a notorious liar who would say anything to get attention.'

'He's also a notorious Gorgon with a massive ego whose worst fear would be looking weak in front of his enemies.' Under the influence of the reaction sensors, SID's tone was less animated than usual. Her waveform remained a subdued rather than fiery shade of red.

'Good point.' Tolbert recalled hearing something about Giorana being the brains behind the brawn of the Empire, so it made sense. The impression he got from his own harrowing encounter with Boss King was that he was a callous bully. There was no way Tolbert would have supplied him with a Universe even if he had one to give. Boss King had already destroyed one of every other Cosmo Dome, except for the Universe. 'Who could have anticipated that anyone, least of all a Gorgon tyrant, would want to keep a set of biospheres that have had their ability to grow taken from them?' he said to himself. 'I didn't invent them to trap life inside a moment and keep in a case to admire.' He wandered up and down in front of shelves of inventions, thinking out loud and then stopped in his tracks staring absently ahead, oblivious to SID's waveform right in front of him.

SID processed quickly but Tolbert hadn't uploaded the game's logbook into System, so she didn't know its full history. She took a moment to respond then gently asked, 'How did it happen?' She could support him better with all the information.

Tolbert didn't want to admit the foolish mistake, but knew it was better to do so. 'A Stop command was mistakenly included in the creation code which made it possible for a Cosmo Dome to be prematurely terminated. I suspect it was out of morbid curiosity that someone discovered that disconnecting the main components preserves the biosphere in that state forever, never able to evolve. It's a tragedy.'

SID's waveform quivered then turned deep purple. After a suspended moment, she spoke softly, 'All life sedated for eternity.'

'Quite possibly. I've logged too many hours attempting to resolve the issue. The one small concession is that it only impacts the construction phase.'

'Life is life,' SID mused.

'Exactly,' Tolbert concurred.

With a lot to process, SID's waveform turned a rich shade of blue. 'Boss King wouldn't sever the biosphere from its power source before it was initiated,' she said after a while.

Tolbert thought for a moment. 'You're right. He would initiate it first. In fact, he would wait until it was fully built before severing it. They're worth more that way.' It sickened him that Gorgon collectors valued severed biospheres over living ones.

'Which means it could be him who has it.'

The beeping beacon continued.

'You can't ignore it,' SID said.

'No.' Tolbert quite enjoyed tinkering away, inventing practical things. The many projects he still had yet to finish gave him a sense of purpose and meaning. He liked seeing the shelves of inventions shift from design to product. Other than the space compactor he was also working on a haulage unit for a local transport company that only needed some soldering and programming and then it would be done. He also had a wellbeing bot, water generator, time machine, threat detector, flora duplicator, and a simulation helmet to conceive. He could ignore the beep and keep the status quo – except he couldn't. Some things you could put to rest, but this wasn't one of them.

'Why do you care so much about an old game?' SID said, again with the mind-reading.

'You're doing that disciplined questioning thing again,' said Tolbert, who knew she cared as much as he did. Life was important to them both.

'Someone has to make you think about your motives.'

'Thanks, but I don't have to.'

'You can't change the past.'

'No, but I can set things right.' Tolbert switched off fans, engines, and anything that made a sound. The beep seemed to come from deep in the clutter, perhaps near the window on the western side.

'It's near the window on the western side.' SID broadcast a coordinate plane with a calculation point of the beacon's location.

'Don't get your hopes up,' Tolbert mumbled to himself. 'It's probably a Jinverse or a Bonverse. Whatever the model, it will be nice to have a new one activated after all this time...' He considered the stacks of boxes and equipment between him and the window and baulked at the mission ahead. The task seemed daunting, but he only had himself to blame.

'You should utilise assistance to move them quickly,' SID recommended.

'I'll be fine,' said Tolbert who thought an activity would help to quell his regrets. He picked up the first box and carried it towards the door.

Before he stepped outside, SID's waveform fluctuated in front of him. 'Without employing assistance, the estimated probability of the day's fulfilment meter reaching green is low to moderate.' If SID could have sighed, she would have.

Tolbert shifted his weight to allow for the heavy box and did his best to determine the pretext of her words. 'If this is about puzzles, then not tonight, SID. I'm afraid I won't be able to focus. Finding the Cosmo Dome mainframe is far more important than entertainment.'

'The game is entertainment,' SID pointed out.

'That's true.'

'But it's more than that.'

'So much more,' Tolbert concurred and stepped outside.

TWO

Mostly Intact

A metallic *thunk!* woke Gelda from her nap. The first thing to cross her mind was that the cleaner had arrived to get the place ready for tomorrow's celebration and had broken something or had an accident. When a muffled voice bellowed a warning, she then wondered if it wasn't the cleaner but the faulty speaker on her voicemail again. Darned thing tended to fluctuate from barely audible to making a raucous noise.

The clock on the wall told her it was almost noon. She cursed herself for falling asleep when there was still so much to do before the celebration. Gone were the days when she enjoyed getting things done. With a groan and a grumble, she brushed grey curls from her eyes and stomped into the kitchen. Preparing to yell at the blasted voicemail, she instead found Finkle the cat rolling around on the floor with a zig-zagged capsule. He held it in place with his front paws while kicking at it with his back legs.

'What have you got there, you big fluffball?'

It wasn't until Gelda noticed a rusted old mailcage beneath the kitchen bench that she figured it out. The biosphere game! Barlo's gift! 'Let go of that, you little menace!'

To Finkle her tone meant *fun!* Kicking off from the item, he skittered out of the kitchen, sending the capsule tumbling in the opposite direction, its pattern giving the illusion of rolling sideways along with forward.

'INSTABILITY HAZARD IMMINENT. SECURE IN PLACE TO MAINTAIN DORMANCY!' blared the same muffled voice Gelda had heard from the living room.

The capsule smacked into the wall; its clasp unlatched. The white in the zigzag pattern flashed red and yellow then four coloured balls tumbled out: green, blue, yellow, and one that flashed black, white, and red. The first three scattered across the floor. The flashing black, white, and red ball vaulted into the air, ricocheted off the wall, hit the metal leg of a kitchen stool, and cracked open to reveal a black pockmarked orb that looked very much like a rock. Dark swirling blues, reds, and purples, and bright twinkling lights appeared from inside the rock for a moment, then it grew dark again.

Though curious, a muffled warning message on repeat took her attention: PREMATURE BIOSPHERE INITIATION! CRAFTING HAZARD LEVEL 9! DISABLE IMMEDIATELY TO AVOID IRREVERSIBLE DAMAGE! It came from the green ball. Turning it round in her hand, the only feature she could find was a small toggle switch that flashed red. Hoping to end the noise, she flicked it and sighed with relief when it worked.

Gelda gathered the four balls and the open capsule and put them on the kitchen bench. The other parcels in the mailbox, and the flashing notification on the screen, confirmed there'd been a delivery while she'd napped. She supposed they'd triggered Finkle's cat senses, which could be unpredictable and hazardous. He had a way of knowing when a collectable was on its way, but his curiosity usually ended in a mess. *Great gosh, the cat's good at breaking things,* she thought. Sometimes she wondered if he were part Gorgon.

When she went to close the flashing ball that had split open, she noticed that the rock inside was cracked. The swirling motions from within made it look as though there were something fluid inside of it. 'Darned cat!' It probably happened when it hit the wall. So much for giving it to Barlo in pristine condition.

She placed the balls in a row on the bench. Judging by the latches on each, they were all containers. She wondered how it all fit together but didn't want to risk damaging it any more.

The capsule sprang open again when she tried to force it shut and she accidentally activated the arrival sequence. The zigzags turned blue and pink. There was some visual noise and a staticky glitch. Unwrap & Play offers spun out in lime green before vanishing in a blast effect on the inside of the lid.

The capsule vibrated; more words appeared:

'Open now for a FREE BONUS!' in bright orange.

'Play today and GET 20% OFF an upgrade!' in vivid purple.

'Sign up a friend and access TEAM MODE!'

'Join our VIP Club! Earn INSTANT Points!'

Across each offer was a flashing 'OFFER EXPIRED' stamp.

'Ugh, Upsells.' Gelda hmphed and shook her head at the crude and obsolete store wrap. It was a miracle the sequence still functioned. She laughed at the thought that she'd bought a product so garishly outmoded. *How gaudy!* The store wrap continued blaring insipid spiels until she closed the lid on the capsule, this time firmly enough that it wouldn't spring open again. The expired deals ended mid-spiel. The zigzags transitioned from pastel through to bright colours, and an illuminated button appeared in the middle of the capsule displaying the word 'ON'. Pressing it crossed her mind but, no, that was Barlo's privilege. She left it off and the yellow faded to grey. Hopefully the woeful store wrap would give him a laugh and the old game inside was still playable.

Wrapping the keepsake brought the ordeal to an end. The high-sensory birthday paper she'd bought from the *Gifting Delights* catalogue had purring cats and fluttering butterflies on it and smelled like fleurs – just like Barlo's baby blanket all those years ago. After adding a green bow, she put it on a high shelf away from Finkle Snook's reach. With a cup of kerai and a slice of swirle bredde she rested and, with much satisfaction, checked 'Wrap Barlo's Gift' off her To-Do list.

For the rest of the day she got on with getting things done. The cleaner cleaned and the gardener mowed while the social screen set to the kitchen wall intermittently pinged with guests confirming attendance, times, what to bring, or to send their apologies. One by one, Gelda checked off items on her list until they were all done. She ate a simple meal while watching reruns of *The Day She Flew*. In bed, she imagined her big empty house filled with cheer and laughter. It gave her an unexpected twinge of anticipation. She had a feeling that tomorrow would be a night to remember and even felt a twinge of nervous excitement. That was something she hadn't felt in a long time.

'Big day tomorrow, Finkle,' she told the cat in the typical soft lilt of her people. Finkle stared at her while she read out tomorrow's list from the biodigital aide device on her wrist. He put one paw on the aide and the other on her lips then closed his eyes.

THREE
Top Priority Job

DIRT CITY, TRONGARL, MIDDLE GORGONIA

It was in Scrapheap District that Ludor finally got to have his deciding brawl. He'd made a bet with himself. If he felt nothing after beating the brains out of a gang of street brawlers, then he would leave Dirt City, bringing closure to his ten lives in service to the Madrik Empire. If the thrill came, he would stay.

He stood atop the mound with a view across the rubble to the Madrik Empire headquarters that loomed in the distance when five – maybe six – brawlers dragged his feet out from under him.

'Your life for mine!' one of them cried out the common Gorgon pre-battle adage in a typical deep gruff voice.

'Bring your best,' Ludor encouraged in a tone void of harshness but still managing to cast impressive conviction, considering he didn't give a fark.

The brawlers dragged him down into the ditch where he

helped arrange them in order from weakest to strongest by knocking them out one by one. All it took was a punch here and a kick there to end it. His knuckles didn't get bloodied, and he didn't even get to use their own weapons on them. Not even an adrenaline rush. They could have jumped down from the dustlands, or one of them could have pretended to be passed out and then kicked his legs out from him for the others to beat up. The whole shitshow was unimaginative, unskilled, and unmotivated.

It was depressingly fitting that such a lame brawl would determine his future. The decision gave him no comfort. Ludor would happily go back to enjoying the farkery if he could, but lately it made him cringe. The tearing flesh and breaking bones, the spilling blood and guts, the pointless loss of limbs and lives... all of it irritated him, and not in a satisfying way. He couldn't fathom his growing aversion to battle. The testing of skill on skill, the lure of victory no longer held appeal. Most weird was he couldn't see the point of it anymore. The total futility of farking shit up for no reason, then more of the same on repeat, was exhausting. Not to mention having to do without stuff or spend time and energy replacing it. The worst thing about it was that he quite liked the peace and quiet, and that was a major problem for someone with the reputation as the most notorious farker around. For one thing, at least, he smelled change off in the distance and it was coming for him.

Head down, Ludor walked on. It was an hour after nightfall, but you wouldn't know it from empty ditchways and carts that weren't even properly armoured. Even with the torches mostly broken this close to HQ, no one lurked in the shadows. Ludor knew the route well enough to make the right turns and search the shadows for the exit. Soon enough, a metal signpost with the Madrik Empire insignia appeared. Faded and dented, it was the same design as the earmarks that locked every employee's DNA to the Madrik Empire.

Ludor touched a hand behind his right ear and recalled the searing pain of the cauterising with the hot iron at the hand of the crown smith novice as the design fused with his skin, and the teeth-rattling throb as the punchgun delivered the small cubic blood transceiver underneath. At the time, becoming part of the Empire offered a sense of place and honour. Now, it was a painful reminder of his poor choices.

The rope ladder out of the ditchwalk had been recently scorched and was too threadbare to use so Ludor dug his fingers deep into the claggy dirt and clambered over the rubble. Most of Dirt City was below ground. Ditchways with rubble walls wound through rundown neighbourhoods of boarded-up squats burrowed into the remains of a once glorious city. Main ditchways were wide enough for carts and people, and ditchwalks were mostly so narrow only a few could walk beside each other before getting shoulders grazed by rock and rubble. Nothing but dust and debris lay above ground other than the Empire's headquarters, the only building still standing in five districts.

Brushing dust from his good pants and clean vest, he walked the dustlands to tall gates in the near distance. They were attached with barbed iron to a fence so powered with impulses a light touch would unmake you from the inside out. It accounted for the mounds of corpses and skeletons scattered around the estate. The gates were the only colour in an otherwise bland landscape. Craned in from an off-world, abandoned Leffel palace, they jutted out from the rubble at different awkward angles making them look like they were about to come crashing down at any moment, which was highly probable. Most of the colour was high up where it couldn't be scratched and sold off. It made the gates look like they'd been dipped in fancy paint.

Ludor had never really paid attention before, but this time something stirred in his belly. It wasn't food or brew, but a *feeling*. It had been stirring a lot recently and Ludor wished it would fark off. Before the feeling, everything had been just the usual unappealing, careless drivel and he'd just sunk right down with them all. Now, he noticed *gates*. Change was almost here.

Ludor didn't stop until he reached the gates. Up close they still loomed large with their ornate twists and curves in soft pastel pinks and greens and the occasional splash of gold, but there were patches of dried vomit, blood stains, and defecation smears. Ludor decided they looked better from a distance.

Dwarfed by the imposing gates, his deputy stood in the gap between them, unmoving. Burgundy-skinned and large, Debrov was a testament to pure Gorgon breeding, in attitude as much as appearance. She didn't turn when Ludor approached. It wasn't that she didn't want to. Her neck was locked in place after she'd lost her head in an altercation. Keen to finish the fight, instead of taking time out to get it stitched back on where it would heal on its own, Debrov had gotten someone to drive a large metal screw into her neck hole so she could fasten her head back on and finish the fight. That her head no longer turned didn't bother her enough to fix it. Her posture was now excellent, though, as was her balance.

When Ludor reached the burly fighter, Debrov inquired in a voice deeper and gruffer than most Gorgons, 'You encounter any brawls on the way over?'

'One. If you could call it that.'

'Better than none. There weren't even any fresh blood splatters on rock, rubble, or dust on my route. It's so quiet everywhere. Not the comforting eery quiet when you sense someone's about to jump you and jab a sword in your neck. No, this is the empty quiet of when no one can be bothered bothering you. Where have the ferocious people gone? All you see these days are weaklings and cowards. We're supposed to honour nightfall, but most can barely stay up until dawn these days. The real issue is that the quiet calms the rage too much.'

Ludor agreed. Trongarl used to suffer passionately and Dirt City, its infamously desecrated capital, was once the centre of chaos, its thorough destruction and exceptional farkery admired throughout Gorgonia. 'You can't stoke the flames of destruction when there's no fire,' he mused.

'What?'

He really couldn't be bothered explaining, but he did. 'It isn't they don't want to, but that there's nothing left to fark up. Look around. There's nothing. Nothing!'

'We still have each other! These bodies are made to break. Let's break them! It sucks not to be invited at knife or gun point into a brawl. Also, where's our usual welcoming party?'

Gangs with bets going to see who could take down the commander and his deputy usually tackled them at the gates but tonight, nothing. Ludor turned his large square head from side to side, checking the shadows, just in case. A dark-brown lock fell across his forehead as he flicked another off his shoulder.

'Your hair is looking particularly voluminous this evening, Commander.' Debrov enjoyed mocking Ludor's choice to let it grow long, down to his chin, instead of shaving it like most Madrik Empire troopers.

'Voluminous? Where'd you learn such a word? Like I've told you, I'll happily cut off a lock for you to keep under your pillow.' He often jested that her scorn was unspoken affection, though most who knew her could verify she was partial to smaller people, mostly women, who in public acted as though they had something to prove but behind closed doors didn't mind being pushed around.

'And like I've told you, I'll happily cut off your head to save your mouth from gushing muck.'

'Spoken like a true driveller.'

The security device hanging from a gate scanned their chips and approved their blood. One half of the gate groaned and shook dirt up from the bit in the ground. The other half swung open and bashed against the fence with a resounding *ting!* They walked to the building that rose from dust and smoke a short distance away.

'Apparently the Challenger is recruiting,' said Debrov who didn't care that her boss preferred to walk in silence.

'I've heard.' He was aware of the rumours. In the barracks, troopers said things. And it was true many were leaving the Empire. Those left behind claimed it was to join the notorious Challenger who allegedly plotted a hostile takeover of the vast Empire that spread across most of Trongarl, bar a coastline of volatile seas. Not that it mattered. Most troopers had gotten fat and lazy since Boss King had been distracted and wouldn't be much use suddenly called back into action, even for a coup. Seizing the Empire was a grand ambition that would put the notorious Challenger in charge of most of Trongarl – if they succeeded. Ludor didn't give two farks. It was a big enough effort to care about the very moment he was in. He didn't even care about an impending future where he offered Boss King a deal that could very well end with his severed head in a jar.

A short distance away, the HQ high-rise emerged tall and

stark against a backdrop of dark smoke. It was a wide and bland building, nothing more than a rectangle with windows, and a pointy column with a large, high-speed security door underneath it. Over the centuries it had endured bombings, fires, and other experimental explosion devices. Now everyone thought it was indestructible. Before Boss King started collecting Leffel artifacts, he had encouraged massive all-out brawls around HQ. Their ruler liked to look out his window and see his people living short and brutal lives, as was the ultimate Gorgon experience. 'Up at nightfall, brawl to dawn, blood-drained and broken, rebirth then go again! Respect the farkery!' had been the cry of many. Now, Boss King's window was boarded up and he didn't care that the dust stayed on the ground instead of being kicked by bloodied limbs. Gone were the piles of lost body parts.

They reached the building without another word. In the security line, they got their earmarks scanned and unloaded their weapons for inspection. With the broken ones replaced, they headed through the security barriers into the foyer to collect their access tags. Eyes darting around, they headed for the executive lift that only top-secret clearance staff used. They kept an eye out for attacks while they waited. There was nothing worse than sitting in a pool of your own blood while in an important meeting. On the mezzanine level, four guards stood around expecting nothing interesting to happen, while three out of five weapon stations were unmanned, and the two troopers threw furtive darts at unsuspecting visitors. Debrov caught one that came her way and threw it back. It landed in the trooper's neck. Smiling down at Debrov, the trooper pulled the dart out and let the blood flow.

'I'll either fark her or fark her up later,' Debrov decided then looked around. 'Now I know why the ditchways are so quiet. This place looks like it hasn't seen any bloodshed for centuries.' This was her first time in HQ since Boss King had locked himself in his office. She eyed up the gaudy artifacts splashed about the place and gawked at a large, stone six-legged hound that took centre stage in the foyer. 'This is some farked up shit.'

It had been a few decades since Ludor had been inside the building and he'd forgotten what an eyesore it was. The vast and varied Madrik Empire collection was now unmatched in Gorgonia. Several impressive statues in the foyer of his 180-storey high-rise included some rare undamaged pieces, and other rarities could be found in the shelves that lined the walls.

'Wait until you see his reception,' Ludor warned as they walked around the mezzanine level to the executive lift.

'Is it true that Boss King has locked himself in a tower?' Debrov wondered. Rumours tended to exaggerate truth, but this was a black or white situation. He either had or hadn't locked himself in a tower.

'You'll see for yourself soon enough.'

Broken statues adorned the walls. Imposing landscape and portrait paintings on the walls had burn holes and rips in them.

'I mean, I get obsessions,' Debrov remarked, 'but broken Leffel crap?'

Ludor shrugged. 'The less there is of something, the more you want.' Debrov's frown told Ludor that he should have kept the thought to himself. More and more lately Ludor worried that he didn't sound like a typical Gorgon. A few centuries back he'd gone through a soft phase and even worried he would rebirth as a Leffel. Lately, non-aggressive thoughts had returned to influence his decisions. Even his skin had an umber tinge to it, appearing more yellow than red when the sun came out, which fortunately wasn't often. 'If there was nothing left to fark up, we'd be farked. We need Leffel shit.'

Debrov grunted. 'Pretty things make you weak.'

Ludor thought of Boss King sitting in his office for centuries, growing flabby while waiting to complete his collection and couldn't disagree. He shrugged. 'They keep the farkery alive.'

Debrov raised a brow as she looked around. 'That explains all the screaming and madness in here. It's a total shitfight.' A sweep of her hand indicated a total lack of activity as far as the eye could see.

'Admins have a no-fight policy,' Ludor explained.

Debrov scoffed. 'You telling me they don't brawl when the going's good? That they do what they're told? Oh, please... Commander, let's straight talk here. People say Boss King's turning so soft he'll rebirth Leffel if he doesn't get back on the job. That true?' Debrov made no secret that she spoke for the squad.

'Collecting Leffel artifacts doesn't turn you into one, dimwit,' he told her. 'Anyway, this stuff isn't worth shit compared to the real treasures.'

If Debrov could have turned her head, she would have done so fast. 'Treasures? What treasures?'

Ludor's need to get one over Debrov always got him in trouble, but she was always so smug. 'All I'm saying is that the early retrievals weren't just about artsy things. Some of their tech can give you the edge over your enemies.'

'What kind of tech?'

Near the public lifts an admin talked with recruits. He

sounded bored as he read from a script. 'If your skin is toned red, your voice gruff, and you can fight off ten enemies at once while remaining nimble and alert, you'll fare well.'

Debrov looked Ludor up and down. 'Yours is more purple than red.'

'And I'm not nimble or alert.'

Debrov chortled. 'You don't have to be. You're the farker. The twenty-meaty-giants tale gets them every time.'

Ludor groaned. 'You're still telling it at the tavern? I keep telling you, they weren't that big.'

He spoke so loud the admin and recruits looked over, then a shower of questions and remarks rained down.

'Commander?'

'The farker?'

'Is it true you've been here for ten centuries? It's a miracle you haven't been head-jarred!'

'You must have seen some brutal shit. I heard you single-handedly annihilated three squads at a tournament.'

That one took him back. It had been a pivotal moment. Fresh off a spacecart from a monotonous world, he'd arrived in Dirt City chasing a better fight. Barely a month later, Boss King had made him commander of the prestigious A-Squad. But that was so long ago, and he was done being owned by the Empire.

Debrov dragged him to the executive lift. They swiped their access tags and up they went.

'What kind of tech?' Debrov asked again.

Ludor grunted. 'The sort that isn't any of your business. Get your head in the job, Deputy. You make me look bad and not in a good way.'

'Is that why you've been demoted?'

'Reassigned,' Ludor corrected, growing impatient. 'I didn't have to take the job.'

'Then why did you?'

'To get away from you squad bastards.'

'Didn't work. I'm still here,' Debrov pointed out.

'Not for long if you can't follow simple orders,' Ludor countered.

'Maybe I'll turn on you,' Debrov threatened.

'Maybe you already have.'

'What's the job?' Debrov asked, changing the subject.

'A retrieval, apparently.'

'We're not trievers.'

'Apparently it's top-level strategic status.'

'Which probably means something lame. This lift's taking forever,' she complained.

'It's a long way up.'

Finally, the lift stopped and the door opened on a large round space with windows all around and a closed section in the middle.

'Fark me, it's a farking tower,' Debrov marvelled, her rough voice turning rougher.

'I thought the long lift ride would have given it away. Go stand rigid somewhere and look menacing.' He barged past Debrov, only peripherally seeing the garish artifacts that lined walls and filled cabinets. There was a striped head on a wooden block and a painting of a blue rock with hammers sticking out of it.

At a desk in front of a dark purple door Naye, the receptionist, sat filing long nails to sharp points. They didn't look up when Ludor and Debrov entered. Ludor leaned over the counter and spoke in undertones, 'Any idea what this is about?'

Naye waved Ludor closer. 'The Leffel toy. He's a farking mess over it.'

'It's for real?' Rumours and speculations had headlined the *Gorgon Gossip* for several years now about a specific model of some long-forgotten fad he needed to complete a collection. Ludor had often wondered if there were any truth to it.

Naye nodded. 'It's beyond an obsession.'

'The job's retrieving a toy?'

Naye shrugged. 'I'm guessing.'

Isn't that just a farking privilege, thought Ludor. He couldn't honestly believe that Boss King had called him up to steal a toy and yet it fit in with all the other bullshit going on around the place. All of a sudden, he had an urge to be alone. If there was a place without people, he would give lives to go there. Maybe someplace with water where he could do something constructive with his hands and walk without a destination.

It would be interesting to make things instead of break them. For anything like that to happen, though, he needed to negotiate his freedom with a tyrant.

Ludor nodded towards the purple door. 'Mood?'

'Impatient, borderline explosive. Your charm may appease him.'

Ludor gave a slight chuckle. Naye secretly listened in on Boss Kings conversations and enjoyed Ludor's wily and precarious retorts, particularly when they crashed.

'I'll show the appropriate amount of enthusiasm and be duly assertive.'

'Maybe ramp it up a notch.'

Ludor pressed his ear to the ID pad in the door. It slid open; he walked inside.

FOUR
Unsuitable Attire

The muffled bleep mocked Tolbert's feeble attempt to make a dent in the clutter. It might as well have cried 'Help!' for the despair it caused him. Sweaty and soiled, he returned to his workstation and, from the many broken mechanical devices on the shelves, chose a house robot recently refurbished for a client. It had a fairly robust crane attachment for a domestic unit.

When SID said, 'You should have activated the house robot from the start to save your energy – and your shirt,' Tolbert didn't react, other than wondering if she was reading his mind again. She was rather fond of I-told-you-so responses, and he let her enjoy them. 'If you had taken my advice, you would already be there.' She couldn't help herself. She had also chosen not to dim her reaction sensors even though Tolbert had suggested she might find it challenging to keep her opinions to herself.

'Always helpful, SID,' he replied, and she was. Mostly.

He patched the bot then mapped a route from his workbench to the Cosmo Dome mainframe. He activated the sequence, and the bot glided to the nearest boxes. It picked them up and slid them onto its built-in lift tray and took them outside, then returned for the next bundle and the next.

Assured that it was up for the task, Tolbert returned to the house where he changed his shirt and made a jova. Back in his chair at the workbench, he ate a scitt and thought about the biosphere game. Those years inventing it had been the best of his past few lives. To this day, it confounded him that he'd successfully grown a new and complex living organism in his workshop. *Cosmo Dome. Those were the days!* As the robot whirred away picking up things with grips and clamps to move them outside (he'd deal with that later), he thought about how good everything had been back then. He'd lived in a nice house in a decent neighbourhood. Weekdays were spent doing what he loved and long weekends were enjoyed with good friends.

The first five models (Jinverse, Bonverse, Thalverse, Wella-verse and Essaverse) had been a learning experiment and were fairly easy to craft. Universe project took his time, energy, social skills, and posture as he crafted day and night. Other than food scouts and home visits from the massage therapist to remedy all the sitting and hunching over, he'd lost contact with the outside world, but he didn't mind. While at times his enthusiasm dwindled into daily grind and a frustrated relentlessness to just get the thing done, he'd never enjoyed anything even close to those seventeen blissful years in the sweet spot of creativity until *ta-da!* there was Universe. With its quirks and surprises, each version was a little different, but they were all truly integrated. His nostalgia faded as he remembered the confounding and unfathomable glitch that had stolen time and energy and too many lives, and still provided no solution.

'The house robot has almost completed the path to the CD mainframe,' said SID.

Tolbert checked the wall clock. The robot had only been at it an hour. His client would be pleased. He got up and stretched his legs, then enjoyed a nice walk through the clutter for the first time in many ages. The path the robot had cleared was much wider and straighter than the narrow winding route into his workshop. It was a much nicer walk that confirmed to Tolbert that more space was indeed a good thing. The window was almost visible behind the last bundle of clutter. The bleep got louder and less muffled. Tolbert paused the bot so he could move everything that wasn't related to the game system into a pile. Using a set of metal pads on the ends of its arms, the robot pressed the pile into an even stack and slid a metal tray under it all. It heaved the lot into the air, backed up, swivelled around, and then off it went without sweating or complaining of a bad back. The beeping grew even louder when Tolbert opened the last remaining box. Though coated in mould and grime, he recognised the Cosmo Dome satchel right away. It had been worth the extra time and troubles making the system compact and lightweight enough to carry around.

The transparent protector shield that Tolbert vaguely recalled using to cover the equipment many years ago was also covered in grime. He peeled it off. The panel was clean and intact, but the tiny lights indicating the locations of the active Cosmo Domes had stopped working. He silenced the beacon then took everything back to his workbench where he repaired broken circuits and replaced a bulb on the panel. He soon had it up and running again.

The featureless white box that was the game's mainframe revealed nothing of its true power. The control panel had so many buttons, dials, and switches to monitor active Cosmo Domes and to assist gameplay, Tolbert now found it difficult to fathom that he'd known them so intimately. The code-board had felt the touch of his fingertips many times a day from the command station in the gaming room back in his former house on his former world. Then, when he moved to Anon, he'd kept the equipment in the back of the workshop for security purposes, a good move as Boss King and his trievers hadn't found it. Not long after their visit, when there was no longer any new activity to monitor, he'd packed it all up, and the equipment had somehow ended up back here.

'CD-Help is still offline,' SID informed.

Tolbert had to manually assess the last reviewed statistics. 'Last check two decades ago there were 387 active games. There were plenty of Jinverses and Bonverses, many Thalverses, a few Wellaverses, not many Essaverses, and no Universes.'

'How many now?' SID enquired.

'368. The missing eighteen are probably either lost, severed, or reset.' He pressed a finger to the DNA receptor and the map came to life with pins of green light. It took a moment to locate the new Active Cosmo Dome pin and Tolbert sighed with relief to see that the light flashed in Leffon. 'It's an Equion address. A place called Alkupera Town.'

'That's not too far away,' SID confirmed. 'Which model is it?'

He alternated between hoping it was the last Universe and hoping it wasn't. On one hand, witnessing a worthy player being the first to overcome the glitch and finish it would be quite something. On the other, Boss King could steal and disconnect it to complete his collection. Tolbert's heart skipped a beat as he pressed the More Info button and then skipped again. 'Universe,' he gasped.

'Told you,' SID gloated. 'The player?'

Tolbert checked the game's stats. 'There's only 0.5 hours of gameplay and 2% played so it's too early for them to assign

DNA.' He fixed a communication error, and Help, the game assistant, came back online.

'A connection cannot be established,' said SID just as he was wondering about it.

'It's probably just a poor reception issue.' His heart racing with the implications of the last Universe coming online, he paced in circles. 'Who has it and why activate it after all these years?'

'The Domers League?' SID suggested.

Tolbert shook his head. He occasionally monitored their club, and the Universe slot in their Cosmo Dome display case was still empty. 'If they had it, we'd know. It has to be a new player.' Tolbert ran his hands through his hair and groaned. 'I have a bad feeling about this.'

'Gorgons aren't permitted in Leffon,' SID reminded him.

'Rules don't stop them.' Tolbert spoke from experience.

'Even it's not him, he'll find it. We need to find out the player's level of competence and their intentions.'

'Without their DNA, there's only one way to do that.'

'Go to them,' Tolbert whispered. More than anything, he wanted to monitor the situation from the safety of his secluded home, but there was no guarantee the new player would assign their DNA to the game and keep playing. Probably the last thing they would expect would be for a Gorgon to knock down their door and steal it, leaving them in a pool of their own blood. No doubt, they'd heal and get on with their lives, but the last Universe would be gone forever. The thought of there being zero chance of a set ever being completed saddened Tolbert. They were all inextricably connected through their time and space. Cosmo Dome wasn't just a game. It was another reality. Universe completed and transformed the set into a greater reality, or so he hoped. The mortals of Universe had more potential than all the rest put together, but the glitch that had destroyed the other twelve versions needed to be resolved. That was another reason to find it.

'Will you go?' SID asked.

Leaving wasn't as easy as just walking out the door. As a long-time recluse, he didn't even know where his outside clothes were, or a hairbrush. Other than workboots for chopping wood and other outdoor activities, having been barefoot for so long, he didn't even know if he owned a presentable pair of shoes. He rummaged through a pile of clothes on the floor of the bedroom he never used and found a pair of musty going-out pants and a crinkled shirt. After giving them a good wash and hanging them in the sun to dry, he cut so many knots from his long hair it ended up short. On the floor in the back of the wardrobe he found a pair of work shoes he used to wear for meetings. With no idea whether he could meet the trends and expectations of the outside world, he put the control panel, mainframe, and codeboard back in their satchel then uploaded the map data into a tracking device.

Ready to leave, he stood looking absently around.

SID read his mind again. 'You have three travel options: book a flyover, trek into town, or use the space compactor.'

'Not a flyover,' Tolbert shook his head emphatically. The last time one came, the pilot thought it fun to perform playful loops and dives into the jungle that made his stomach churn and his head spin. 'Trekking into town will take too long.'

'That leaves the compactor,' said SID.

'I haven't run the final test yet.'

'You've tested it seven times. Eight if you include the time you accidentally switched it on. System reports that it's stable.'

'And your assessment?'

'Ninety-seven percent effective. It's the size that's an issue, but it's just you so it won't be a problem.'

Tolbert stood undecided. He had successfully sent inanimate objects and discarnate beings through but nothing alive. It seemed risky.

'There's minimal risk,' SID reasoned. 'You're the inventor.'

It was a timely reminder. It had always been his view that the first to try something should be its inventor and here was his chance.

'Yes?' SID understood that sometimes Tolbert knew the answer and just needed a push.

He took a moment longer to be certain and to gather his nerves then said, 'Yes.'

Unwrapping the space compactor from the filmshield Tolbert took a moment to stabilise it then checked it over a final time.

'I'm mostly convinced.'

'Then you're ready.'

'Not quite.' On the wall near the door, the semiconductor lights of System's control panel flashed in rhythmic patterns. The hum of its steady processing soothed and assured. Only once had it been moved and that was from its place of origin to Anon. For the trip, Tolbert had made a mobile version so that SID was able to assist with the move. The outside world had been such an overwhelming experience that she had turned her sensors down even though the flight was short and uneventful. Now, Tolbert opened the source box wedged into the wall behind the panel, took out the mobile attachment to the side of the mainframe, and activated it.

'I'm coming with you?' SID's waveform flickered hints of red.

Tolbert paused programming the mobile system. 'Of course.'

'Outside?' The red-blue waveform quivered.

Tolbert couldn't fathom facing the mission without her but didn't want to put her through a sensory overload by taking her into the complex world of people, activity, and things. 'If you feel the pressure too much just turn down your sensors. If it's still too much, you can withdraw to sleep mode.'

There was no answer for a long moment, then the waveform settled somewhat with brief moments of flickering red while remaining mostly pale blue. More than anything, SID liked to be useful and needed. 'I've estimated there is a slim chance that I'll struggle, a moderate chance that I'll enjoy it, and a high chance that I'll be useful. You need me.'

Tolbert smiled. 'I do. You're valued, SID.'

'It's important to be valued.'

'Agreed. It makes everything better.'

The conversation ended when Tolbert split System from full to mobile capacity. He selected the extracted data he needed to run the game and SID's functions then left the rest intact. After programming the mobile system, he strapped the compactor to his waist and set the coordinates to Equion.

'Are you there, SID?' he asked, when he turned mobile system back on.

'I'm here,' she said. Her voice was quieter and her waveform shorter.

'Good, good. Let's go then!'

Hoisting the satchel over his head and under one arm, Tolbert strapped the space compactor to his chest and activated it by pressing buttons on his aide. Swirling colours rippled across its surface then faint transparent rings pulsated out and back in, warping the space ahead.

'Estimated time to full charge is unknown,' SID announced.

'Hmm. Some things you just can't predict, but we'll know for next time,' Tolbert replied. He watched the pulsating rings intensify until they warped space like rings of water from a thrown stone.

'This way is open,' the compactor's vocal decoder said on repeat between two long pauses filled with bleeps. The large button in its centre flashed a lit-up green 'Open'.

'Time to go!' Tolbert took one last look around then left his remote home in the Merlavin cloud forest for the first time in over a century.

FIVE

Mint Green, Turquoise, White, Gold

The weather was often perfect in Alkupera Town, but it was extra perfect on the day of Barlo's last rebirthday celebration. The sky was clear, and a fresh breeze drifted in from the Loloho Sea. People walked with two- and four-legged friends. Delicate winged insects fluttered around bright fleurs that bloomed in gardens. Bells on food carts jingled as they released billowy clouds of sweetness into the air, enticing people from slumber. It was the loveliest of lovely days until tomorrow, which could quite possibly be even better.

Up since dawn with the day's To-Do list in hand, Gelda was dressed and had eaten a substantial breakfast in the hope of getting through a day that held no promise of a nap. Calls were made and messages sent; the kitchen and lounge room were tidy. She was double-checking that the bathrooms and bedrooms were presentable when the door chimed.

'Tawawa, Raquin!' she sang to her daughter as she opened the door. The customary Leffel greeting, typically delivered sincerely and passionately from the heart, meant, 'Hello! I love you! You're amazing! May your life be fulfilling!'

'Tawawa, Ma!' Around boxes held in both hands and bulging bags slung over each shoulder, Raquin embraced her mother.

Gelda saw herself in her daughter's large golden-brown eyes, wide forehead, and pointed chin. In contrast to Gelda's long grey curls, Raquin had cut her dark hair so short her locks had gone. While Gelda kept fit enough with aquadance and stretcharobics, she didn't dedicate herself quite as much to class as Raquin did to rock-climbing and so she was nowhere near as toned and strong. She most likely didn't look so fresh and healthy either.

'It's a special day,' Gelda said as she prised a box from under Raquin's arm to ease the load.

'So special. Can you believe my baby has lived a thousand years?!' Raquin exclaimed as she heaved the bundle past Gelda into the house.

'It is quite something!' Gelda still found it miraculous that they'd both had the privilege of motherhood. It was especially rare for two consecutive generations of women to be so fortunate for their birth centuries to include, not just their own chance at life, but also another's. It was an honour and privilege they respected.

'Tawawa, Gelda!'

Gelda turned back to the doorstep. 'Tawawa, Hazzy!' Their long-time family friend had kindly offered to cater the special event. Though only reaching to Gelda's chest, Hazzy didn't struggle under the weight of the tower of boxes she gracefully balanced while still managing to bend her head around them to offer the warm greeting. Her strength and suppleness was that of someone twice her size. Gelda had often wondered if Hazzy's bones were made of something tougher than hers.

Gelda took a box in her free arm, and they followed Raquin into the kitchen where they unpacked all the goodies. The kitchen quickly filled with colours, and smells as they began chopping and arranging. Appetizers, mains, and desserts emerged on the kitchen bench as they created dish after dish, chatting away while their aides pinged on their wrists with messages and reminders.

Everything was going along splendidly until the blender broke. Raquin frowned. 'Things are still breaking?'

'At this point, I'm surprised when something actually works.'

'Oh, no. What else?'

'Where do I start? The toaster, mailbox, kettle, blender... The taps leak, the rubbish chute clogs, and Finkle's litter tray constantly stops emptying. You can imagine how much fun that is.'

'Gosh, darling,' said Hazzy. 'That's just so odd! And you've had them fixed?'

'Several times. I simply don't have the energy to bother with it all anymore. Oh, and now my aide is on the blink. It's stopped receiving commands and rarely delivers my notifications.' She held up her wrist to show the flickering screen.

'Have you reset it?'

'Constantly. Now the darned thing only works on manual mode. I've resorted to using voice and touch commands to get anything to happen.'

'That's so weird everything breaking at once,' said Hazzy.

'Why haven't you said anything before now?'

Gelda shook her head with a sigh. 'I don't know. It's just so...'

'Annoying?' Hazzy offered. 'Infuriating?'

'*Persistent*,' Gelda blurted then forced herself to settle down and put the issue into perspective. 'There was no point in telling you. The whole situation is merely a reflection of my own state of collapse.'

Raquin stopped decorating pouflins and offered a hand to her mother who took it to comfort her daughter more than herself. 'Oh, Ma. You're barely ten thousand lifetimes old! So you're a bit stuck right now, but it will pass.' She worried for her mother and couldn't understand what held her back from rebirthing. 'I always find the best remedy for exhaustion is to do something invigorating.'

With slumped shoulders, Gelda wrinkled her brow. Raquin hadn't lived enough to understand how, as the centuries pass, lives blend until you wake one day to discover that there's nothing new to do. It was about experiences not lifetimes. The irony was Raquin needed to live more lives to understand that. 'If only it was that simple,' she said.

'It is, Ma. You need a new hobby, something different and challenging. Why not join a club?'

'What sort of club?' Gelda had been a member of so many common interest clubs, she couldn't imagine there was one she hadn't considered.

Raquin thought about it. 'You love quizzes and puzzles, or what about a new sport to foster more energy? Playing cards? Drama? Games?'

'I've tried them all. Speaking of games, I bought Barlo a

biosphere game for his rebirthday. Darned cat knocked it off the bench so it might be broken, but it's more of a commemoration gift.'

Raquin chose her next words carefully. 'It's not another Marvellus novelty, is it?'

'It's not a novelty. It's an old biosphere creation game from his birth century. You know how he loves growing things in his spare time.' Barlo was a professional worldmaker and liked to develop microworlds to raise unique organisms on his days off. 'This is a little different, but he's going to love it.'

Raquin tried not to make a face. 'I'm sure he will, Ma, but his biospheres are complex environments, not games.'

Gelda shook her head. 'Cosmo Dome *is* a complex environment – just inside a game.' She frowned upon realising that she wasn't certain of the fact but said nothing of her doubts. Raquin's doubtful expression clearly revealed she needed persuading. 'At least take a look before you deem it unsuitable.' Gelda fetched the gift from the shelf in the lounge room and unwrapped the purring cats and fluttering butterflies paper. It released a floral scent too delicate to survive the baking and frying smells in the kitchen.

When picked up, the grey zigzag pattern turned yellow. The crack down the middle seemed wider and longer than earlier, giving the case a scruffy, second-hand look. Gelda carefully opened it so Raquin could see the four coloured balls inside and indicated the flashing one. 'I think that's the biosphere.'

'Why's it flashing like that?'

'Finkle.'

Raquin sighed. 'Then it's probably jinxed.'

'He's a good cat,' said Gelda, even though she had her doubts about the origins of his breed. More and more, she doubted he was pure Leffel.

Raquin's brow lifted in disagreement, but she said nothing.

Gelda sighed. 'Perhaps Barlo is too sensible to see the funny side of the old thing,' she said absently. 'He probably wouldn't be interested in playing it.' Now that she thought about it, a biosphere game wasn't suitable at all. 'Maybe you're right,' she conceded. 'It is a bit unremarkable.'

From arranging the last frosted pouflin on a tray Raquin looked up, smiled and nodded. 'Why don't you go in on the trip like we originally planned?'

'Yes, I will.' When they'd first started planning the celebrations, Raquin had proposed they get Barlo a Trip of a Lifetime Package Deal but Gelda had insisted on finding her grandson something exclusively from her, hoping it would bring them closer. Now she worried the old game would do the opposite. She put the capsule back on the shelf to deal with later.

As they finished preparing delicious delights that they arranged on plates and platters and into bowls and jugs, Bryll, Raquin's dear friend and surrogate father to Barlo, arrived.

'Tawawa, Bryll darling!' Gelda held him close then pushed him away to get a good look at him. 'Is that what you're wearing tonight?' Bryll had on a pair of loose dark pants and a pale blue shirt.

'Tawawa, Ma Varda!' He beamed. 'Have you ever known me to dress down to a party?' Unzipping a bag, he showed her a gold pantsuit with a flashy turquoise-and-white belt that matched the theme perfectly.

Gelda laughed. 'You'll be so well camouflaged no one will

notice you.' The decoration colour scheme was mint green, turquoise, white, and gold.

'Oh, they'll notice me,' Bryll assured her with a wink. 'What about you, Ma. What will you wear?'

Gelda gasped. 'My outfit! It totally slipped my mind and didn't even make it onto my list!'

Eyes and mouth wide, Bryll looked positively aghast. 'You haven't chosen an outfit yet?'

Gelda thought about the racks of unworn dresses in her wardrobe and considered what it would take to feel presentable. A gown could only do so much. If it could make her feel lively again, it would be a miracle. 'I'm sure I'll find something,' she told him.

Bryll shook his head repeatedly. 'Oh, this won't do!' He dragged her into her changing room. His head darted from side to side as he swished hangers of frocks and pantsuits along rows of racks. 'No, no, no. These are all too straight up and down and too bland for a such a special occasion. Ma Varda, tonight you must sparkle.' Gelda sat on the bed, watching as he dug deeper into her wardrobe. At the very back, Bryll found a silver gown she'd bought for a ball many eons ago that she'd never attended. It had sequins on the neck band and a purple velvet sash around the waist.

She tried it on, and it fit quite well. The sequins gave it a shimmering look and rippled when she moved.

Hand to chest, Bryll softly squealed. 'Oh, I am so good at this!'

They laughed. Gelda kissed Bryll's cheek. 'Thank you, darling.'

'Now take it off and come help me decorate.'

Gelda changed back into her day clothes and went back downstairs to find her ex-husband, Barlo's Grandpa Odgio, wandering towards the lounge.

'Oh, there you are!' he said when he saw her on the stairs. He wore a slimming black suit with a bright red bowtie and carried a red box with a black bow. He'd been enjoying matching colours in his clothing, home décor, and anywhere he could do so for quite some time.

'Tawawa, love.' He kissed Gelda lightly on the cheek. 'The elixir barrel is around the back.'

'Delightful! Your recipe?'

'With some minor improvements. It's still made from fuliana leaves but fermented a little longer for a smoother taste.'

'I can't wait to try it.' Gelda didn't often enjoy the intoxicating stimulant that was served at most parties, but Odgio's elixir had just enough flavour and plenty of vitality. He had recently studied elixary and was discovering a hidden talent for refining unnoticed flavours and distinctive tones. 'Did you bring your faceted decanters?'

'It's the only way to drink it,' said Odgio. The self-chilling unbreakable glass decanters with heavy bases and fine-rimmed tops were custom-made to keep his popular elixir refined. The brims and conical shape kept the bubbling liquid inside so you could sip at the coloured vapours first.

Bryll appeared carrying a box of decorations. 'Tawawa, Odgio! You're just in time to help decorate!'

The three of them transformed the house into a wonderland. They hung tapestries, arranged large paper fans and filled vases with extravagant fleurs, then displayed interactive signs and hung salutations and snapshots of Barlo throughout the house. Outside near the pool they allocated a spot for gift-giving and hooked up speakers and cascading lights in an area perfect for dancing. What tied it all together and turned it into a wonderland was the white table setting that Hazzy and Raquin created with turquoise floating lights in front of each place setting, and mint green fleurs suspended from the ceiling by gold thread.

'Barlo's going to be speechless when he sees all of this,' Gelda marvelled and they all agreed.

The afternoon passed in a flurry of last-minute preparations. Raquin and Bryll left to get ready and pick up Barlo, while Hazzy decorated a cake she'd baked the previous day. The servers arrived and were given instructions then asked to help set the table. The grand event was soon ready to receive guests, with an hour to spare.

As Gelda sat in her chair to have a short rest, she felt a twinge of anxious anticipation. This was about when she usually took a nap. Hazzy caught her yawning and winked at Bryll and Odgio.

'The party hasn't even started yet and she's already pining for her bed.'

'In my defence, I've been up since five and haven't stopped,' Gelda said with another yawn. 'Gone are the times when I could last a day without a nap.'

You could say anything to Hazzy and she would laugh, which she did. 'How long has it been past your rebirth now, sweet-pea?' she asked.

Gelda shrugged. 'Somewhere around ninety years,' she esti-mated. 'I stopped counting after fifty.' She had almost dou-bled a lifetime waiting for newness, and it still eluded her.

'You might have Ebb Syndrome,' Hazzy informed her. 'It happened to my aunt. She lived large for ten lifetimes, then nothing interested her for centuries so she went to the wilderness.'

'The wilderness? Really?' Gelda didn't know anyone who'd been and come back to talk of it, other than news and entertainment reports that gave the impression that only bold voyagers went on such mysterious adventures, not aunts who spent too much newness in one go then had to suffer through a few boring lifetimes.

Hazzy nodded eagerly. 'She came back bursting with newness. Apparently, it's not what you would expect. "You don't find newness. It finds you," my aunt told me. That's what you should do, Gelda.'

'Go to the wilderness?' If she had the energy and inclination, adventure would be a fine thing.

'No, let newness find you,' Hazzy clarified.

'It can find me right here in Alkupera Town,' Gelda said.

'Oh, sweetie, try being more carefree!' As an optimist who enjoyed graceful lives that flowed from one lovely experience to the next, Hazzy didn't understand how Gelda could be stuck.

'Ma Varda doesn't do carefree,' said Bryll. 'She's good at finding things and solving puzzles though.'

'And cracking mysteries,' Odgio interjected.

'Then you have plenty of reasons to rebirth!' said Hazzy and threw her arms around Gelda and squeezed tight as if wrapping her dear friend in her own surplus gaiety.

In soothing tones that cast joyful vibes, the four friends

chatted for a while then went to get dressed.

'It's nice to dress up once in a while, isn't it?' said Gelda when they met up again downstairs. From head to toe they glittered and gleamed.

The doorbell chimed and Bryll cried out, 'Let the festivities commence!'

SIX

Mildly Appealing Deal

When Ludor entered Boss King's office, it was as if he'd opened a garbage disposal that hadn't been cleaned out in quite some time and things had gone from decaying to growing into other things. He'd been places where lost limbs and body parts were piled high and left for months and the smell wasn't as bad. What stood out the most in the stuffy room was a large box-shaped stain on the oak wall, surrounded by a myriad of paintings with ornate frames that decorated that and every other wall in the office. The stain matched the size and shape of something covered by a clean, white sheet that took up most of the space on the matching big old oak desk below it.

The rest of the office was a testament to how a person could exist in a small space without cleaning it for decades and still be alive. A sagging couch that had been a bed for quite some time draped dirty sheets and a lumpy pillow across what was once a green-grey carpet and was now stained in shades of brown, red, and specks of black (probably rot). Ludor thought he saw a few fungals growing in a corner. He definitely saw a few roaches scurry away and a large rat scamper off into the adjoining ensuite, probably to feed its many offspring.

Last time Ludor was inside the office it had been a simple, uncluttered place of work – other than the expanding collection of Leffel stuff. He hadn't noticed a smell, good or bad.

Boss King wasn't immediately noticeable behind his desk, but the bad smell seemed to come from that area of the room, and Ludor thought he heard a low raspy breathing, so he bent his head around the desk and there, amongst the jumble, was the infamous ruler. This was the first time Ludor had seen him in over a decade. Twice a year the commanders met with him in the boardroom to discuss defence matters. Those meetings had stopped decades ago.

Staying inside an office for ten years could change a man. Gone was the burly leader who demanded attention. In his place was one who couldn't even sit up straight, let alone dodge a bullet. Ludor took a few steps towards the desk. A man who resembled an obese slug that spilled out over a large chair watched him. His hair and beard had grown out and, without care, had become so knotted and wily he looked like low-level security. Made to break, their official look communicated a clear message: 'Come at me. I have nothing worth living for.' Except Boss King did have something to live for and Ludor was about to find out what that was.

Naye had warned Ludor that Boss King had let himself go and only showered and changed his suit every other week. 'I had to force him into it by threatening to let as many of his enemies inside HQ as I could find.'

This is the before and after pictures in reverse, thought Ludor. Granted, Boss King had always been a little different to other Gorgon leaders, such as enjoying the finer things in life. 'Class is rank,' he often said. 'That's how I stay on top. Suits and ties, bowler hats, and walking canes show your enemies that you're better than them.' At one point, Boss King had his trackers working on getting him a crown and claimed all would bow before him once he had one. But it had clearly destroyed him. Clearly getting farked up over nice stuff wasn't as remotely rewarding as farking shit up. There was nothing thrilling about this. It was just sad.

'Your Royal Sir,' said Ludor with a low bow.

Boss King acknowledged him with a wave of a hand and indicated the chair across the desk from him. 'Sit, sit.'

Ludor sat and positioned the chair so he could see Boss King through the gap between the processor and the covered thing that took most of the space on the office desk. Since last time they'd met, Boss King had really let himself go. The ID tag around his neck that he never took off linked his DNA to the building and to the fate of everyone who worked for him. It was the only thing on him that sparkled, though only mildly. He looked like he'd barely slept or eaten in weeks. Frankly, he looked like shit.

'You look like shit,' said Ludor. He was the only one who spoke with Boss King so casually. He got away with it because Boss King thought of him not only as his Commander, but also his confidant. Probably because Ludor was the only person who could handle Boss King's volatile dispensations. It was mostly a matter of necessity and somewhat of apathy. He had demanded Ludor be blunt with him at all times, and so he was. Ludor considered the crumpled papers, scattered folders, and random stationery that hid the rest of the desk from sight in the spots not covered in dirty jova cups and plates fuzzy with mouldy food. A computer lay dusty and neglected and pushed to one side.

'Stop judging me.' Boss King glared at Ludor through the gap.

Ludor raised his hands in mock surrender. 'You're pretty judgeable right now.'

'Fark you.' Boss King stared hard at Ludor then softened slightly. 'Your next assignment is probably the most important one of your lives, maybe all of our lives. It's confidential, top-level-as-fark security, and requires you to travel to Leffon.'

Great, just *great*. Leffon was the last place anyone would want to go, especially to find a toy. *How did I end up here?* he wondered, about to undertake the dullest assignment of his career. 'Sounds intriguing.' He sighed.

'You could at least show a little interest.' Boss King grumbled. 'Maybe this will help.' He raised flabby arms into the air and smacked them into the arms of his chair to propel himself up. Steadying himself, he hoisted to a standing position and gave his legs a chance to settle. With a surprisingly graceful sweep, he pulled the sheet away from the rectangle thing to reveal a rather fancy glass cabinet with brass frames. 'Ta-da! My biospheres, severed to perfection!'

Ludor lifted a brow. While the strange rocks were kind of interesting, what with their colours and patterns, he had to admit the shiny cabinet that held them was quite impressive. 'Nice box,' he remarked.

'It's a *cabinet*. It's some of the finest craftmanship you'll ever see. The frames are solid gold from the ancient Zenzi mines. Worth a fortune! It's even got DNA biometric authentication to stop random farkers from opening them.'

There were two rows of three impeccably planed glass cubes. Each cube had a hinged door that opened from a delicate handle. The frames shone, the glass gleamed.

'You wouldn't know it from its pristine condition, but it's a classic piece of storage furniture. It's clearly only ever been owned by people who appreciated it.'

Ludor nodded. It certainly stood out in the big old dirty office in a tower in a big old dirty high-rise on the wrong end of town.

Boss King took out a cloth and began polishing it. 'I like to see inside it at all times.' He gave a sweep of his hand to indicate the contents of the fancy cabinet. 'So. What do you think of the biospheres?'

'The what?'

'The things inside, farktard.'

Each glass cube except one contained a dark rock on a stand. Each had a slightly different hue and pattern on its surface, but they were all clearly part of a set. Each stand had a name engraved on it.

'What do you think? They're from an old Leffel video game called Cosmo Dome. All the savvy VIPs want one. They're worth more than worlds.'

'What's the big deal?' Ludor asked.

Boss King glowered. 'You want your head jarred or something? The big deal is they've been severed.'

'So?' Ludor had no interest in hearing details unless they helped to find the stupid thing.

'*So?*' Boss King bellowed indignantly. 'That means they'll stay this way forever, which makes them twice as valuable as unbuilt ones and thousands of times more than built ones. Try and get your tiny brain around *that*! Severing isn't easy. It can only happen before they're built, and you have to choose your moment wisely to stop them at their prime. It's a *skill.*' He tapped a pudgy finger at the cabinet. 'Each model you see here contains a different assortment of organisms that have been suspended in time. There were once alive. Imagine! It took ages to find one of each almost fully made. Six models make a set. Most people only have one, but I'm better than most people obviously. When I first started collecting them, I smashed heaps. You'd never believe how boring they are when they're only just started, but almost finished they're *incredible!*' He jabbed a finger at Ludor. 'What you are witnessing here, Commander, are perfectly preserved moments in time and space. This is art at its finest. This is beauty.'

Though Ludor had no idea what all that meant and no interest in finding out, he nodded along in agreement. All he needed to know was what the missing one looked like and how to find it. As Boss King wiped his finger-mark off the cabinet, Ludor thought he detected a gleam in his eye and wondered what was going on inside his head. Once obsessed with ruling and oppressing, and destroying those who didn't obey, now he seemed to have completely lost interest in being the best at being the worst. If he didn't get back on track soon, his days were numbered. Ludor hadn't wanted to believe it, but clearly Boss King had lost it. While Boss King rambled on, Ludor heard just enough to prove it as he ranted and raved, repeating himself.

'My collection is the best in Leffon and Gorgonia, probably in all the worlds. Discerning collectors would give worlds to get their hands on a complete set of unique and impeccable biospheres. Security is imperative as you would imagine, which is why I keep the door locked and the biohazard alarm activated...'

While Boss King blathered on, Ludor waited impatiently for a gap to ask for something back. It was fair enough after ten centuries of service. A moment almost presented itself when Boss King stopped speaking, but then his eyes grew dark. Ludor's eyes followed his attention to the top left empty cubicle. Ludor knew he couldn't admit to reading the *Gorgon Goss* so he settled on asking a simple question that would hope-fully not exacerbate his boss' wrath. 'Lost or stolen?'

Boss King's mind wandered. 'She knows me. I shouldn't have married her. I shouldn't have stayed married to her.'

It took a moment for Ludor to realise Boss King meant his ex-wife, Giorana. 'You shouldn't have slept with Zondu.' Ludor shrugged off, regretting the words.

Boss King's eyebrows went down for a second and then way up. He laughed. 'So you know. She wasn't charming like Gio-rana. Her tricks were crude, but a fark's a fark, right?'

Ludor's patience was rewarded when Boss King blurted out the story. 'I don't know where or how she found a Universe – they're super-rare – but she faked an auction for it then anon-ymously outbid me with my own money.'

'After she found out about Zondu?' Ludor asked to confirm but Boss King wasn't listening.

'Then she sent a picture of the Universe listed on some Leffel marketplace and marked it sold. The bitch *traded* it! The most farked up thing about it was she didn't even care about the fark. It was because Zondu took her farking precious orange slingbacks.' The scowl came back deeper than ever along with a slow shake of the head. 'There were no other bidders. None!'

Ah, the shoes. So the rumours were true. 'But you got them back off Zondu, right?' Not even the best *Goss* reporters had uncovered exactly what had happened, and Ludor was curi-ous enough to ask how the shoes were returned. Zondu was notoriously greedy.

Boss King gave a laugh devoid of humour. 'At a price.'

'What did she want?'

'The mansion.'

Ludor laughed. 'Bold move. What did you give her?'

'The west coast manor.'

Ludor thought for a moment. 'Isn't the leveller due to hit there again soon?'

Boss King smiled. 'Next month.'

'So, you gave Giorana her shoes back in return for the toy?'

Boss King gave a sullen nod. 'Bitch cut the straps off and said, "Oh, darling, how sweet of you, but they went out of season thirty years ago".' He spoke in a high voice and dragged out the words to mimic Giorana. I told her if she didn't tell me who she sold it to, I'd shrink her brain and toss it in the sewer inside an iron bearing.'

'Ouch. How'd she take that?'

'Said something about how I always resort to mindless violence. Like that's supposed to be an insult? She also said there's no way I'll ever finish my collection. I'll show her. Universes don't come along often, you know. I searched for three centuries. The last one was two centuries ago and it withered a year after I severed it...'

As Boss King trailed off in another ramble that involved showing his pictures on his aide, Ludor thought about Giorana. In all his years working for Boss King, Ludor had never met her. He'd seen her every day since his first, but only from behind as she slipped away from the high-rise early in the evening or when she came back early the next morning. All he knew was that her skin was more purple than red and she wore her ashen hair tightly pulled up into a coil on her head. Despite the break-up (or maybe because of it), she still came to HQ every morning and left every evening. Rumour was the Empire was built on her fortune, from old money. She only ever seemed to wear grey and black tailored suits, but she matched her accessories in one bright colour that changed weekly. This week her shoes, handbag, and hat were bright blue. She timed her arrivals and departures so proficiently that in the ten centuries he'd worked for Boss King, he'd never once had the chance to introduce himself and find out what she looked like up close and in person.

'Commander!'

Ludor looked up. 'What?'

'I said I need you to go to Leffon and get my Universe.'

'The toy?'

'It's a collectable.'

A *collectable*. Instead of managing armies he was retrieving a toy... in farking Leffon. There were plenty of other troopers better qualified in retrievals, such as Captain, which he now mentioned with slight resentment and without thinking.

Boss King shook his head so fast his jowls wobbled left to right. 'That farktard's only interested in accolades. I need someone I can trust to get the job done fast, which is why I'm sending you. Do we have a problem here?'

Ludor suppressed his ego and reminded himself this was a chance to get out. 'No problem.'

'Good, then get me my Universe.

Boss King swiped and tapped at his aide then thrust his wrist at Ludor. 'This is what you're retrieving.'

It was an image of a rock that to Ludor looked just like the others. 'It looks just like the others.'

'Are you blind? It's got more colours, forms, and textures. Look closer and you'll see moving swirls amongst vast darkness. They're galaxies.'

Ludor didn't know what a galaxy was, but he looked closer anyway and saw nothing that interesting.

Boss King sent him the image then said, 'The trackers were supposed to report back yesterday. Naye says they're confirming coordinates. Trievers are ready and waiting.'

'How many?'

'As many as you want.'

Boss King leaned forward so his chins were almost resting on the table. 'I don't care what you have to do to get it, just get it. Commander, you're the only one I trust to do this. You're loyal and everyone respects you.'

Except for my deputy, thought Ludor, *and probably my squad, too.* If he was totally honest with himself, Boss King's assumption about his allegiance wasn't particularly judicious, considering it was Gorgon nature to betray, rebel, and do whatever it took to win, but that was the nature of bosses.

The buzzer buzzed. Boss King grunted and pressed his hand to it. 'What?'

'The trackers are back,' said Naye. 'ETA an hour.'

'They've found my Universe?'

'Seems so. In Equion, Leffon.'

Boss King gave a smug sigh and fell back into his chair with a smile. 'I'm going to have a reveal party. No, a gala. I'll do it in style.'

'Sounds good. When's the last time you looked in a mirror?'

'Why?'

Ludor leaned over and pressed the buzzer. 'Naye, bring in a mirror, would you?'

A few moments later, Naye appeared carrying the ornate mirror that usually hung in the foyer. Ludor placed it between the display cabinet and his boss.

'Fark. I look like security.'

'Get a large, extra-strong shower gel and a new scrubber,' Ludor told Naye. 'And get on to the barber. Tell him to bring the shears.'

'I'm on it!' Naye had been waiting for a long time for something to do besides tell people Boss King was 'currently unavailable.'

Ludor stood but didn't leave. This was his only chance to speak his wishes before he went to find the toy. Once he found it, Boss King wouldn't let him go. 'Always negotiate your terms before you deliver the goods,' he often told his squad. He would follow his own advice.

'What are you waiting for?' Boss King snapped at Ludor. 'Go get my Universe! And make sure you get it before it gets built, otherwise it's useless to me. None of those useless farkers out there can tell me if it's being played yet, so I can't tell you how much time you have, so the sooner you leave, the better your chances of keeping your head. *Go!'*

Ludor couldn't go. It was the most inopportune moment to speak up, but it was the only chance he had. 'I'll get the toy for you but I want something in return.'

Boss King's eyes darkened. 'What?'

Ludor made sure not to hesitate. 'My release pass.'

Boss King, on the other hand, hesitated for quite a while. 'You want out? Is this some sort of blackmail bullshit?'

'No blackmail bullshit. I've been a commander for ten centuries and now I want to explore other opportunities.'

'Explore other opportunities?! I've given you everything, you ungrateful farktard! You want a promotion, is that it?'

'Status doesn't interest me. I want change.'

'Then force a rebirth or take timeout in a fun den. Don't waste my time with your whining... Get the fark out of here!'

He should have known. Empire troopers didn't earn release passes. The crown used them as leverage for acts above and beyond duty. Being good at his job sucked. The thought of being stuck on Trongarl indefinitely felt like tight hands around Ludor's neck. For a moment he forgot about his own options and thought about Boss King's. If the retrieval was urgent, he was in a prime bargaining position. 'You don't have time to find someone else.'

'I could take your head.'

'And lose the toy.'

'It's a collectable!'

'Whatever. Do we have a deal?'

Boss King glared harder as he considered it. 'Fine, quit. I'm tired of seeing your ugly face anyway. Go and earn your precious freedom! Farker!'

With his eyes firmly on Boss King's hands, Ludor backed out.

'Freedom, my arse! You'll be begging to come back!' He could still hear Boss King rant and rave after he'd closed the door. It used to be the only thing that Ludor cared about was lifting the cloud of disappointment that hovered over him day by dull day long enough to down a few brews and drown his sorrows. He could run classes teaching how to lead a rotten life. But now, the only thing he cared about was getting his pass. When he placed the Leffel toy on Boss King's desk, that's when change would arrive, and he'd greet it with one question: 'What the fark took you so long?!' And he would laugh his way to Trongarl's gates.

Back in reception, Debrov marched up to him. 'Trackers are back and ready to hand over intel to the trievers. Both parties are waiting for your orders in the common room.'

'You've been busy.' Her ability to get things done was why Ludor put up with her shit.

As he led them out, he turned to Naye who looked up from booking the barber and frowned. 'What?' they snapped.

'Have you ever seen Giorana?'

'Duh. Only every day.'

'Describe her to me.'

'She's...' Naye frowned. 'Um, I guess she's not very memorable.'

'Or you've never seen her face.'

As Ludor left to meet the new squad, he heard Naye say, 'So weird.'

When Ludor told Debrov about the job, she repeated everything in disgust and disbelief. 'He called us up to strong-arm a toy for him? Fark me! He might as well hand the Empire over to the Challenger tied in a red farking ribbon. To be clear on this: we have to retrieve it before it's built so he can stop the thing from evolving and enjoy one farking moment of it forever? That's peak level pathetic. And it's in Leffon? Fark me! Have you been?'

'Not since the split. You?'

'Not likely. Could be fun farking up new shit though.'

Ludor grunted. 'No diversions. We get in and get out.'

Debrov exaggerated his grunt. 'What's the point of trashing and bashing if you don't enjoy it?'

'You're right. There's no point at all,' Ludor agreed.

The lift pinged; down they went.

In Basement Level 2, in a room made of iron and clay, two separate groups sat at tables eating large meals and drinking from stone mugs. The trackers were smaller with dark-orange tones to their skin. They spoke quietly between eating reasonable portions of food. The trievers had dark reddish-purple skin and shovelled overloaded spoonfuls of food towards their large gobs, missing more often than not. The only person to look up when Ludor and Debrov entered was an average-sized trooper with short grey hair on his head, cheeks, and chin, known only as Captain.

Debrov addressed him. 'Farktard? Please tell me you're not on this job.'

'Someone's got to keep these farkers busy,' he replied. 'What the fark are you doing here?'

'Boss King sent us. Seems you're doing a shit job.'

Captain glowered at Ludor. 'That true?'

Ludor gave him a curt nod. 'Yep, you're doing a shit job.' He turned from Captain and got the attention of the trackers and demanded the intel. An unusually small, dark-orange trooper hurriedly pressed some buttons on their aide and shortly Ludor's pinged. He read notes and coordinates then said, 'Trievers, follow me.' Plates and mugs smashing, the squad lugged themselves up and trudged after him.

Perhaps they might move faster on empty stomachs and while dehydrated, Ludor noted. He got them to line up and hoped at least a few of them would present their best. They were a disorganised bunch. A rough headcount was around twenty-three.

He did a few quick psych tests and picked four troopers based on their ability to follow orders and think clearly under pressure.

'Only four?' Debrov asked.

'Quality over quantity,' Ludor replied. His greatest weakness was seeing the good in people. If he could replace Captain, he would. The sly bastard was notoriously defensive and resentful. Whenever they were on a job together, he questioned everything and deliberately went against orders. With any luck the four trievers weren't that loyal to him.

'Find a way to Equion,' he told Debrov.

'Already sorted,' said Captain. 'Anything else, Commander?' He literally spat the title.

Ludor glanced over at the trievers who were back shovelling food and drink in their mouths. 'How about you get them on task?'

Captain slapped them around a bit then dragged them back over. He shoved them in chairs facing Ludor who sized them up. Retrievers were named according to categories assigned by their trainers, with number codes to represent their grades in relation to others in their class. SHARP-9S21 was smaller than the rest and despite their name didn't look like they'd win an intelligent contest. At least they weren't covered in food like FORCE-9F17. Enormous and gruff, his bare back was covered in smutty sketches. FIERCE-9FI06 had a shaved head that exposed a knobbed scalp scattered with scars. One arm was on backwards and her head had that recently re-grown shine about it. BRISK-9B11 was the only one not eating. She looked reasonably fit and agile.

Fed and rested, weapon sacks on backs, the four trievers stood waiting for orders. When Ludor told them the plan was to go to Leffon to retrieve a top-secret artifact, they went into a frenzy thinking of all the new first-rate stuff they could fark up, from appliances and apparel to vehicles and buildings.

'Uh, Leffels,' Captain reminded them, which significantly lowered their enthusiasm.

'They're gunna wanna hug un talk about *feelings*,' complained

SHARP.

'They're gunna wanna be *friends*,' grumbled BRISK.

'Them's so soft in voice and ways makes me wanna puke,' whined FIERCE.

'Ugh,' FORCE remarked insightfully.

Finally, Debrov had had enough. 'Shut your gobs, you bunch of whiners.'

'Let's get this thing done,' said Ludor. 'Where's our ride?'

'In the basement,' said Captain.

'What kind of ride is kept in a basement?' Debrov asked him. 'You'll see,' was all Captain would say as he led them there.

SEVEN

Party Games

By the time the warm glow of dusk brought an end to the day, Gelda's house in Alkupera Town was bursting with people in fancy and fabulous attire chatting, laughing, drinking, and eating delicious appetizers presented on gold trays by smiling servers. While Gelda only knew a handful of the guests, she was glad Barlo had plenty of people to help him celebrate.

When everyone was onto their second drinks, Raquin announced the arrival of the rebirthday boy fresh from his recent rebirth and the last he would officially celebrate. In a sparkling purple jacket and shiny yellow pants, he shone inside and out.

'You look so refreshed!' said a guest.

'I have so much energy and focus!' As if to prove it, Barlo swirled around the room and heartily received hugs, back slaps, and kisses to a soundtrack of whoops and whistles.

'Tawawa, Barlo!' guests sang out. 'Enjoy your last rebirthday party!'

'Tawawa!' Barlo laughed and laughed.

When the welcoming was over, he looked around at the decorations and food, then joined Gelda, Raquin, Bryll, Odgio, and Hazzy who stood between the dining and lounge rooms watching the goings-on.

'It's a wonderland!' Barlo exclaimed and graciously thanked everyone who helped.

Raquin handed him his favourite drink in a gold mug she'd sculpted especially for the occasion and Barlo went off to enjoy the merriment.

Dinner was nine petite courses of fried, baked, pickled, and raw cuisine arranged into designs on white plates. An oddly pleasing mishmash of flavours, colours, and aromas perfectly reflected the occasion. Compliments flowed towards Hazzy who beamed with pride.

After dinner, everyone gathered near the pool, gifts in hand. Barlo stood in front of them all and one by one guests handed him wrapped items. He shared a moment with each as he opened them. The last gift was the Trip of a Lifetime ticket wrapped in a long thin box. Watching Barlo's speechless reaction, Gelda decided she'd made the right choice by not giving him the game. That is until, sometime later, when Odgio called out to her from the lounge room.

'I was leaning against the shelf when Finkle leaped onto my shoulder and pawed it off.' Odgio held out the capsule that contained the abandoned rebirthday gift. 'I caught it just in time!'

It had turned red again. Gelda looked from the capsule to Finkle who sat at Odgio's feet waiting for him to drop it. He rolled on to his back with his cute paws bent up in the air, staring innocently at Gelda, and gave a sweet little meow.

'He really wants it.' Odgio laughed.

'Darn cat's too smart,' said Gelda with a shake of her head and a smile.

Finkle got to his feet and looked voraciously up at the capsule. 'Don't even think about it,' Gelda warned. He slumped onto the floor, rolled over, and pretended to stretch while still looking at it, gaining nothing but a laugh from them.

Gelda took the capsule from Odgio and put it back on the shelf where it turned grey.

'Aren't you going to give it to Barlo?'

She shook her head.

'Why ever not?'

Gelda reluctantly told him what it was. 'I got to commemorate his birth decade, but it's old and broken.'

'Let me see,' said Odgio, reaching towards the shelf.

'Oh, another gift!' Hazzy appeared, clapping her hands.

'It's old and broken,' Odgio repeated.

'What is?' Hazzy enquired.

'A game I was going to give Barlo. It's nothing, really,' Gelda said.

'Did someone say game?' said Bryll, heading over to see.

'What game?' asked Hazzy.

Before long, Gelda was surrounded by people wanting to see it. She thought twice about opening it to show them the four mysterious balls inside. Perhaps another day, after she'd rested from the party, but their enthusiasm was unrelenting. Though Barlo was nowhere to be seen, she sat in her chair and put the capsule on the lounge table. Eager guests huddled around her. Some sat on the sofa, while others pulled up chairs. Those that missed out on seats, sat on the floor or stood around her. When everyone was settled, Gelda opened the capsule to reveal the balls.

'What do they do?' Hazzy asked from between Bryll and Odgio on the sofa.

'They're containers,' Gelda replied.

'You haven't opened them?' asked Odgio.

'No, but one of them broke and there's a rock inside. I think it's the biosphere.'

'A rock? Is it a Cosmo Dome?' said Bryll hopefully.

'It is.' Gelda gave him a curious frown.

'Terrific! I haven't seen one in centuries!' From his seat on the sofa, Bryll leaned forward to see it properly. 'Biosphere games were all the rage back then. Cosmo Domes were the best. I had a Thalverse. It was enchanting!'

'Oh, I remember those,' recalled a guest standing behind the sofa.

'My brother had a Wellaverse but didn't even finish building it,' said someone else.

'Some models are pretty rare these days,' Bryll continued. 'Collectors go mad for original editions.'

Hazzy leaned in for a better look. 'The case looks pretty old. It could be an antique and might be worth something. My friend collects old games and has exhibitions in museums. She frequently gets offers from collectors.'

Everyone had an opinion to share about the different Cosmo Dome models. Elixirs in bellies meant they possessed varying degrees of reliability.

'Is this the game that was in the news recently?' Odgio asked.

'Yes, something about a notorious Gorgon collector and some drama with his ex-wife?' said Bryll.

Already under the influence of Odgio's enchanting elixir, everyone's favourite aunt Fansy joined them. She nudged Bryll, Hazzy, and Odgio along to sit on the sofa. After they caught her up, she shook her head. 'These things are dangerous. There was a guy who got his head blasted off when his world imploded. People shouldn't be able to make biospheres without credentials.' Being a woman who liked to use her hands to display words, she cheerily sloshed elixir around.

'Rubbish,' said Odgio, narrowly dodging splashes. 'Biospheres should be created for fun. Everyone takes things too seriously these days.'

'Slow down, everyone. I've never seen one before so I'm struggling to keep up,' said Hazzy. 'What's the deal?'

'You build a biosphere – that's a type of mini world – and keep it alive,' Bryll summarised.

'Sort of,' said a woman who stood to the side of the small crowd.

She had large green eyes and a streak of hair to match and was wearing a casual dress with a bold botanical pattern and boots. Gelda thought it seemed an odd choice for a party, but then some people didn't like dressing up. She didn't know who she was. She'd only met Barlo's close friends, and there were many people she hadn't met in attendance.

'They're all a little different,' the woman explained in a soft voice that was gentle yet commanding. 'Some are more complex than others, but the general idea is to create lifeforms and help them to survive and thrive.'

'So, it's just growing things,' Fansy presumed. 'Sounds boring.'

'Not at all,' replied the woman.

Guests in front of her moved aside and Hazzy made room at the lounge table. The newcomer received both gestures by approaching the table and sitting on the floor where she tucked her dress under her thighs and continued to talk with calm authority. Though all eyes were on her, she didn't seem to notice. 'You get to create billions of lifeforms then make them survive and thrive, some under the harshest of conditions. There are six models to choose from and they're all a little different. Some only have a few elements while others are more complex.'

'You seem to know a lot about Cosmo Domes,' she said to the woman. 'Did you also have one?'

Though a simple question, the woman hesitated before answering. 'I've spent a lot of time around them.' Her short laugh seemed forced, and Gelda thought it must be nerves as she wasn't the least bit awkward.

'What's your name, love?' asked Gelda.

'Shellany.'

'Tawawa, Shellany!' everyone said and gave their names in return.

'Is the rock the biosphere?' Gelda asked once the introductions were done.

'You've seen it?'

'When my cat knocked it off the bench. I think it's dented.'

Shellany's mouth dropped open then shut quickly. She shook her head. 'The rock, as you call it, is the preservation chamber for the biosphere inside.'

'Open it!' a guest urged.

'Yes, let's see the biosphere!' Hazzy clapped her hands.

'You can't actually open it, as the preservation chamber is a self-contained bionetwork, but we can see inside it. Shellany reached for the capsule. 'May I?'

'Of course,' said Gelda. 'Lately I seem to have a knack for breaking things, and you seem to know a lot about these.'

Everyone crammed in close to the lounge table to get a look at the mysterious game. Some sat or crouched while others stood behind them. Raucous laughter from beyond the room reminded Gelda that there was a party going on – a party she hosted for her grandson. She wondered if Barlo was having a good time. As the host, a sense of obligation to check on guests conflicted with a desire to stay and play until she reminded herself that people would find her here if needed. Guilt eased, she sat back in her chair and watched.

Shellany opened the capsule and took out the four balls. Swiping a hand over each revealed a single white word on each in bold ornate type. The blue ball had *Mainframe* on it.

The green had *Controller*, the yellow *Components*, and the one that flickered between black, white, and red read *Chamber*.

Upon seeing the flashing ball Shellany asked. 'What exactly happened?'

Gelda explained how Finkle knocked it over and it came out of the mailcage and how it hit the wall and cracked.

'And he's a black cat,' Hazzy added.

Shellany glanced thoughtfully away then said, 'Cosmo Dome biospheres are fragile, but they can also be quite adaptable. Selecting the yellow *Components* ball, she twisted it open to reveal several small connectors, a pin board, and two different sized discs. The larger disc was white with dulled-out lights that went all the way around its edge. The smaller disc was black with a button on one side and a port on the other. Shellany attached the pin board to the black disc then connected the two joined pieces to the white disc. 'That's the powerstation set up,' she said then opened the ball with the biosphere in it.

Gelda noticed Shellany's eager expression fade when she took it out and saw the crack. 'I hope it's not broken.'

'Me, too.' Shellany carefully positioned the biosphere chamber on the powerstation. It clicked into place on the pins. 'And there you have it: the Cosmo Dome,' she said with a flourishing wave of her hand. 'A biosphere inside a preservation chamber, kept alive by a powerstation.'

'Why isn't anything happening?' Fansy said.

'It's not connected yet,' replied Shellany.

She took out the blue ball with the label *Mainframe* and twisted it open. Inside was a smaller white ball with diamond-shaped grooves on its surface. She pressed a diamond that was slightly more raised than the others and the whole thing expanded outwards and turned into a large white box with three buttons on one side and a large convex lens on the top.

Everyone oohh'd and aahh'd.

'The mainframe processes calculations and transactions,' Shellany explained. 'It also analyses information and converts into a readable format.' She took a connector from the yellow components ball and attached the mainframe to the biosphere chamber.

The green ball twisted open to reveal another white ball, but this one had hexagonal-shaped grooves on its surface. Again, Shellany pressed a raised shape and it expanded outwards. It turned into a white rectangular apparatus slightly larger and thinner than the first with dials, buttons, and a gauge screen on the top. 'This is the main controller.' Shellany pointed at several icons on the right. 'That's your equipment. It's press-activated.' Gelda recognised a wheel, a blaster, and some sort of visor.

Shellany took the last big connector from the yellow *Components* ball and attached the controller to the biosphere chamber. The last pieces in the components ball were four small connectors. Shellany inserted one into a port on the Cosmo Dome powerstation and another into a port on the controller. A visible energy wave travelled between the two, turning from pale white to vivid blue.

The small crowd oohh'd and aahh'd again.

Shellany then flicked a large switch on the mainframe that lit up green. The same muffled warning message Gelda had heard the previous day started to play on repeat.

'PREMATURE BIOSPHERE INITIATION! CRAFTING HAZ-ARD LEVEL 9! TO AVOID IRREVERSIBLE DAMAGE, DISABLE IMMEDIATELY!'

Everyone groaned at the booming voice. Fansy put her hands over her ears.

'That can't be good.' Bryll winced.

'It's not ideal,' said Shellany.

'I thought I switched that off,' said Gelda.

'You may have temporarily disabled it,' Shellany suggested.

'Which is why I shouldn't play.' Given her recent track record for breakages, Gelda worried she would make things worse.

'Your game, your responsibility,' Bryll sang with a sassy grin.

'It's not mine,' Gelda reminded him.

'What she means is she's afraid to try new things,' Odgio teased.

Beyond being offended, Gelda laughed. 'It's not really my thing.'

'Have you ever played a biosphere game?' Bryll challenged. When Gelda shook her head, he added, 'Darling, you don't know what you're missing!'

'Maybe you can keep it as part of your own collection?' Hazzy indicated the cabinets full of Marvellus figurines.

'Yes, do that,' said Hazzy.

'It's not a collectable,' Gelda and Shellany said in unison then shared a soft smile.

'Maybe Barlo might want it after all,' Gelda said.

Shellany shook her head. 'You've already activated it, which means you're its creator.'

'Technically, the cat activated it,' Gelda joked. She'd already thought about selling or giving it away, but for now the responsibility of pressing buttons fell to her apparently – if only to ensure it was working.

She flicked the switch on the mainframe next to the large convex lens.

A small square white display appeared above it with the spoken warning almost verbatim in blue type: *Premature biosphere initiation... Crafting hazard level 9... Avoid irreversible damage... Disable? Yes, No.*

'Press *Yes*,' Shellany instructed.

The *Yes* option lit up under her finger when Gelda pressed it to disable the premature initiation. There was a hissing noise from inside the chamber then the previous message was replaced by a confirmation message and a new query: *Construction Mode Recovered. Enable Normal Operating Mode? Yes, No.*

'Disaster diffused,' Shellany announced as she fell back into the chair with a sigh of relief.

The small crowd cheered.

Hazzy squealed. 'Phew!'

'Your streak of bad luck is over,' said Odgio.

'Don't jinx it!' Bryll worried.

'So that's it?' enquired a confused Fansy.

'As far as the initiation goes, yes,' Shellany told her. 'Now it's set up to play.'

'Is it playable?' Gelda wondered if it was okay. She forced herself to relax the tension in her body which, she realised, held more excitement than fear.

'It looks stable. The biosphere initiated without the control system in charge. Hopefully it hasn't evolved by itself.'

'It's only been a day,' Gelda told her.

'A lot can happen inside a biosphere in one day,' Shellany replied. 'The only way to tell for certain is to play it.'

'Yes, play!' Hazzy cried out.

Gelda laughed. 'I'm not sure if I'm ready for that.'

'Of course, you are!' said an eager Hazzy.

'We should see what model it is,' said Shellany.

It took a few deep breaths to quell her second thoughts. The four to five party elixirs she'd consumed numbed any apprehension she might have otherwise experienced. She sat upright and pressed *Yes* to the *Enable Normal Operating Mode* query.

Shellany showed Gelda around the controller then got her to press buttons and turn dials until the lens on the mainframe console lit up. There was a short whirring sound, then light splayed out from the convex lens. Flourishes of red, yellow, blue, and every colour in between burst out filling the air above the mainframe, then vanished, leaving behind a deep blue glow that dressed the room from floor to ceiling in perceived infinite depth.

Expecting something big to happen, the small crowd grew silent. Accompanied by suspenseful music, from a pinpoint of light somewhere in the middle depths grew the words *Cosmo Dome*. In a detailed and vividly coloured animated font, the words spun around several times, separated, twisted away from each other, then returned to smack together with a bang. As the music ascended with accelerating rhythms animated objects exploded in every direction that vanished on the outer limits. After a slight pause, *Universe* appeared underneath in a bold, gleaming gold font, zoomed close, then disappeared in a feathery eruption.

The small crowd cheered.

'It's a Universe!' Gelda cried out. She turned wide eyes towards Shellany who looked oddly relieved. Everyone else whooped and cheered. Elixirs sloshed in the air as everyone in the small crowd got excited over the unveiling. Gelda was, too, until a worrying thought came to mind. 'Isn't that the hardest one?' she wondered.

'It's more tricky than hard, but also super rare,' Shellany explained. 'The Universe is the most complex and breathtaking biosphere of all the Cosmo Dome models. Yours has been prematurely initiated, and the fall may have caused issues, but you're extremely lucky to have the greatest and most advanced biosphere that's ever been invented.' She grew suddenly serious. 'We can't let anyone harm it. It has to be protected.'

As Shellany's words trailed off, Gelda got the impression that her mind had briefly gone elsewhere. Her grave tone muted the sense of excitement in the room. Gelda looked around to see everyone staring at Shellany with mild concern and thought it time to intervene. 'Absolutely,' she said in enthusiastic agreement then waved her hands to indicate the spectacle before them. 'This is just so incredible!' It broke the tension, wrinkled brows smoothed.

Shellany offered a conciliatory smile. 'The Universe model has sophisticated worlds called planets,' she explained, though no one asked. 'You develop the habitable ones and foster advanced civilisations. With enough resourceful ingenuity they evolve into a harmonious ecosystem.' She took a long pause. 'I recommend that you play the construction levels so it's protected from further harm. Will you play?'

Gelda wasn't sure. She considered the display before her. The Cosmo Dome branding was now at the bottom right of the display under a help icon, just above a potted plant near the window. On the bottom left was a small white button that read *Play* in bright green and *Pause* dulled out. While the rest of the display presented nothing but black space, she was left with the impression that it went on forever. She wanted to know more about what the demo had shown, but what had started out as fun now felt almost like a burden. If she had known the game involved protecting living beings, she might not have agreed to play. She wasn't comfortable admitting that, though, so instead she merely confessed, 'I don't know what I'm doing.'

'Universe has a superior AI who is helpful and pleasant,' Shellany assured her. 'The construction stage won't take too long. After that, if you decide not to keep playing, you can surrender it to the Domers League. They'll happily look after it for you.'

'It has its own club!' exclaimed Hazzy drawing murmurs from all.

While exhausted, Gelda's other main concern had nothing to do with losing sleep and everything to do with recent events. 'What if I break it?'

'It's failsafe and I'll be here to assist.' When Gelda remained quiet, Shellany added softly, 'Honestly, I understand your concerns. It's a big responsibility, but there's nothing like playing Cosmo Dome for the first time. It's so rewarding and the Universe in particular is really quite spectacular to see fully built.'

'Imagine the fun you'll have creating tiny worlds!' said Hazzy. 'You love puzzle games and you're caring and sensible. It's the perfect pastime for you!'

Aware that everyone waited for her, Gelda suddenly found herself wanting to vanish so she wouldn't have to decide. The prospect of playing made her nervous, and caring for squillions of worlds when she couldn't even get her appliances to work seemed a bit much.

'What are you going to do with it, Ma Varda?' asked Bryll.

Odgio gave a wink. 'A party isn't complete without a game.'

There were murmurs of agreement from the small crowd. 'Play it!' someone cried out.

'Grow some lifeforms!' Hazzy sang out.

'This could be your path to newness,' Raquin said quietly in her ear.

They're right, thought Gelda. Something new and different could be just what I need. Something fun. Cosmo Dome could be just the thing to kickstart a new life.

'Play, play, play,' Bryll chanted.

'Play! Play! Play!' everyone joined in.

Gelda wasn't a showy person, nor was she much of an entertainer, but with everyone staring at her expectantly, she didn't have the heart to say no. 'Okay, I'll play it!'

EIGHT

Scent of Departure

In Basement 1, Ludor stood with Debrov, Captain, and the four trievers, wondering what they were looking at. Inside a cell, something white and fluffy slept huddled in the corner of a dirty and blood-stained mattress.

'What are we doing here?' he asked Captain. 'Where's our ride?'

'In front of you,' Captain replied with an eyeroll.

'Mutt!' called BRISK.

Startled awake, the hound lifted its head. Upon seeing the Gorgons, it flinched then pressed itself into the corner of the wall, quivering as if trying to shrink or become invisible. If it had eyes, they weren't apparent. One ear was black like half of its face. A grey strip ran from somewhere near the top of its head to a tiny nose. A tail emerged from billowing fur to sluggishly waggle.

'Is that a hound?' Debrov asked.

'Mostly. Sometimes is portal,' said SHARP.

'It's a portal host?' Ludor had heard of bioportals but had never believed they were real, especially one that was part hound.

Debrov took a step forward. 'How does it work?'

'Not well very,' said FORCE. 'Lots we've tried, from whipping to belt beating on noggin, though not wants to obey. Instead pees, bleeds, and whimpers.'

'What does work then?' Debrov asked but no one answered. The mood in the basement turned awkward.

Ludor sighed. 'We don't have time for this, so someone tell me how we get this thing to... open?'

'You does must be nice,' said SHARP quietly, and no one spoke for several long moments until Ludor demanded, 'Unlock the farking cell!' When it was open, he stood with nothing but space between him and the hound to see what it would do. It turned out to be nothing.

'Does it have eyes?'

'Yes.'

'Will it attack me?'

The trievers laughed. FIERCE said, 'It's a weakling boofhead.'

'Come here,' Ludor said to the hound in his usual forceful tone.

Its ears disappeared behind its fluffy head.

'Here, Mutt,' said Ludor in a softer tone, using the name

BRISK had called it. The hound sat up on the bed and offered a demure expression but still avoided eye contact.

Ludor slapped his thigh. 'Come here. Come on,' he said in a friendlier tone.

Mutt's ears pricked. A tail waggled timidly. With caution, the hound stepped off the mattress and approached Ludor who knelt and patted the ground. 'That's it,' he encouraged while fighting an urge to add, 'I won't hurt you.'

It took some coaxing but eventually the hound crawled to Ludor who held it while Captain attached a chain to a collar that had metal balls dangling from it. They took the hound into the courtyard where SHARP unhinged one of the balls from the collar, put dirt in it, then closed it again.

'What's with the dirt and balls?' asked Debrov.

'To open spacegate, hound needs scent of departure site and coordinates of destination site,' SHARP explained.

Ludor accessed a map on his aide and recited the coordinates to SHARP who turned tiny dials on the active ball with her large hands. When it glowed piercing light blue, Mutt grew agitated and didn't calm until he got to sniff it. SHARP let him off his chain. 'Go! Go! Go!' she said and the trievers all threw soft things for the enormous pooch.

'What lame level of farkery is this?' Debrov said and continued to curse over the situation though no one paid her any attention. Not that she cared.

'Have to play to open.' FORCE's scowl was part embarrassment and part anger.

'What the fark is happening?' Debrov grumbled. 'We're watching a bunch of trievers act like Leffels to get a hound portal open so we can go steal a farking toy. It's shameful, Commander. Farking shameful.'

Ludor wondered if playing with a hound was fun until its mouth grew so large it took over its face. Its hair grew long and twisted around a face that was more of a gaping hole with a tongue for a walkway.

'What the farking fark?' Debrov said.

'Let's go!' said Captain.

The trievers heaved their weapon sacks on backs and looked to Ludor to give the order.

'Through that?' Debrov pointed in disgust. The bioportal was a slobbery and slippery vortex that smelled like wet dog.

Captain ignored her. 'You'll want to give the order soon, Commander, otherwise it'll close.'

'Let's go!' said Ludor and led the squad through the bioportal.

NINE

For Training Purposes Only

Gelda didn't get to play Cosmo Dome right away.

Not realising how much time had passed delving into the captivating game, she went for a quick bathroom break and found that the party had quietened down. Feeling awful for abandoning her host duties, she made up for it with belated attention to remaining guests. Most congregated in the kitchen with Raquin and Barlo.

'This has been the best rebirthday party ever, Grandma!' Barlo declared when he saw her. With a tight hug he asked, 'Have you been enjoying yourself?'

'So much.' Gelda beamed and told him about the game.

'It sounds like a blast!'

'It is! I haven't even started playing yet, but already it's like nothing I've ever experienced. It's quite challenging, too.'

Barlo gave a confused frown. 'Have you just been playing in demo mode then?'

Gelda shook her head. 'Not even. There was an initiation issue, but your friend Shellany has been helping.'

'Who?'

'The woman with the green streak in her hair?'

Barlo thought for a moment. 'Oh, *her*. I assumed she was one of *your* friends.'

'No. That's odd. Oh, well. I'm sure there's a reasonable explanation,' Gelda replied, though she couldn't think of one. Now she was even more curious about the mysterious yet helpful guest.

'Someone's plus one probably. Anyway, I want to see this new Marvellus game of yours!' Barlo gushed and promised to join her soon.

Before returning to the game, Gelda retreated to her room to lie down for a moment. Having a house full of lively people was a refreshing change but exhausting. These past few centuries, it was rare for her to have anyone over at all. When she did, it was only three or four friends. From lethargy more than choice, she spent most days other than Bingo on Tuesday mornings alone with Finkle and the entertainment feed for company. Most evenings she was in bed by nine, except for Friday when she went to a movie or played cards with friends.

On the bed, Finkle slept. His eyes narrowly opened when she stroked his head. 'My sweet boy,' she soothed and snuggled up next to him. Purrs soothed.

Eyes closed, tight muscles eased, she drifted into a light doze while the muffled sounds of the remaining guests down-stairs added a distant comfort. Ten minutes of rest would revive her for another few hours. She found herself smiling. Hosting a large party wasn't too bad. Everyone was having a good time, even her. These days, that was indeed a rare thing.

Leaving the cat to his haven away from boisterous elixir-infused humans, she headed back downstairs. In the lounge room, an animated spectacle that filled the air above the lounge table and splayed onto the rear wall took her breath away. *Demo Mode* flashed in semi-transparent lettering over-top scenes that looped through enticing snippets of game-play. Gelda imagined herself zooming through dark space observing in close proximity the strange objects in all shapes and sizes as they moved and changed. *What a wonder!* She grew increasingly excited to know more, especially when a close-up of an enchanting planet showed simple organisms evolving into complex sophisticated species.

An overlay, translucent enough to see through, appeared in the air before her. On it was a coin meter making clinking sounds. When full, it burst and more life exploded. She won-dered what was going on. *The demo mode does a fine job of lur-ing a player in*, she decided.

Her attention leaving the spectacle, Gelda stepped into the room to find the remaining guests huddled around the lounge table watching another game that had begun in her absence. Elixir decanters were piled up on the other end of the table from the Cosmo Dome setup forming the rough shape of a pyramid without a top.

From the sofa where she sat with Hazzy, Fansy slurred, 'Who drank all the decanters?' while groping the air next to a cooler stacked full of them.

'Not me. I'm still quite sedate, actually,' Hazzy said, then tripped over the cooler while reaching around the table to a lower spot on the pyramid. She somehow managed to position a decanter perfectly.

The small crowd cheered.

'What are you all doing?' Gelda wondered with a giggle as she leaned against her armchair where Bryll was sitting.

'Tawawa, Gelda!' said Hazzy upon noticing her. 'We're playing elixamid! Get it?'

'On account of the shape of the decanters *and* the structure,' Odgio mansplained with a slur.

'Bets are on whether they'll make it through the drinking to put the last decanter on top, or if the elixir effects will bring it crashing down,' said Shellany who sat in one of two dining chairs opposite the sofa someone had brought in while Gelda was resting. While her wry smile revealed she was amused by the game, her attention kept drifting to the virtual display.

From the other dining chair, Odgio chuckled. 'It could go either way.'

For the moment, Gelda brushed aside curiosity about the identity of her mysterious guest and watched the game.

Bryll grinned while attempting to position a decanter on top of Hazzy's. He missed the table altogether and fell into a fit of laughter. With only a row or two left, and with a somewhat steady hand, Odgio went next.

'Careful,' warned Fansy sloshing elixir about.

'Hey!' Hazzy wiped her damp cheek.

'Keep still!' said Bryll, managing to place another decanter on the towering structure.

'Let's finish so we can watch Gelda play Cosmo Dome!' Hazzy suggested.

Turns came and went; somehow the increased pace warranted better moves. With only one decanter left to go, they argued over who would take the turn.

'What about Gelda?' Shellany suggested to unanimous agreement.

Gelda examined the structure, noted its weak points, then very carefully positioned the final decanter on top. It wobbled, lingered steadily for a brief moment, and looked like it would stay – until Fansy jumped up with premature excitement. Her knee caught the edge of the table sending the structure crashing.

'*No!*' everyone cried out as decanters tumbled across the wobbling table and onto the floor.

Shellany's reaction was immediate and effective. One hand steadied the table, while the other stopped the Cosmo Dome controller from sliding off it.

'Good save.' Gelda exhaled in relief and wondered once again about the mysterious guest's reasons for being here. *She's probably someone's plus one like Barlo said.* She decided not to worry. Without Shellany's help, the game would still be unactive and thought of as broken.

'I rate that a success!' said Hazzy and high-fived anyone who cared to smack her raised hand.

'What happened?' Fansy wondered and they all laughed.

After they cleaned up, Gelda got settled in her armchair and rearranged the gaming equipment back on the table.

'Cosmo Dome time!' Hazzy clapped her hands.

Everyone's attention went to the looping demo-mode game-play in the air around them. When Gelda pressed the dia-mond button on the controller, the demo disappeared. Complemented by a pleasant melody, the *Cosmo Dome* brand-ing lifted from the bottom right of the display and tumbled to the centre, then exploded leaving behind dark space with a flashing, illuminated blue diamond. Shining resplendently in white light within was the word, *Begin*.

'Before you begin, I'd recommend you switch Help on,' Shel-lany advised.

'I definitely need it,' Gelda murmured and pressed a finger to the icon hovering above the potted plant. The overlay appeared again. This time it held a query: *Enable Help? Yes, No*. In smaller type below was *Help is an intrinsic component the Cosmo Dome System (CDS)*.

Pressing *Yes* triggered soft music then a pleasant voice from the controller speaker. 'Tawawa! I am Help, your game assis-tant. What shall I call you?' When Gelda said her name, Help replied with, 'I am delighted to make your acquaintance, Gelda. Let's begin. To qualify to play Cosmo Dome, first you must submit your DNA. The Cosmo Dome system enhances your DNA to foster maximum diversity. In the Universe model, it is transformed further to carry out the complex functions needed for thorough evolution. Please press a fin-ger to the button on the powerstation.'

Shellany pointed out an inconspicuous spiral-shaped but-ton on the front of the powerstation below the preservation chamber. It turned red when Gelda pressed it, flashed white a few times, and then turned a steady green. '*DNA approved*' appeared with a brief uplifting sound then vanished.

'Congratulations! You're in,' Shellany said with a gentle smile.

Help explained what everything was for and pointed out features. Since Shellany had already told Gelda most of it, she instead took a moment to admire the setup. Everything looked so old and yet somehow advanced. 'I've never seen anything like it,' she murmured.

Help zoomed in on dials, gauges, screens, and buttons, then a second overlay with a query appeared: *Enable Training Mode? Yes. No.*

'I definitely need training.' Gelda looked to Shellany for confirmation. 'Don't I?'

Shellany looked up from her aide with a slightly concerned expression that disappeared quickly. 'What? Oh, yes. Definitely.'

Gelda briefly wondered what had taken Shellany's attention then took her own back to the game. Gentle rhythms started when she pressed *Yes* then the black backdrop shrank to a pinpoint and vanished. It was replaced by an environment that appeared similar to a scene in the demo mode Gelda had watched in autoplay earlier, except more abstract. The overlay read *For Training Purposes Only.*

'You are now viewing a simplified simulated model of the Universe biosphere,' Help explained

Gelda plugged in one of the two remaining power connectors to remotely connect the steering wheel to the preservation chamber. A steady blue energy current stretched between them.

Pulling the hovering steering wheel down to her lap in both hands, she became familiar with the colour-coded speed settings arranged in a ring on the control pad. Pressing the up and down buttons under her thumbs, she traversed the simulated cosmic scenery of the training arena, crawling in red then creeping in orange towards virtual galaxies. Soft rousing music steered her onwards. She cruised in yellow, coasted in green, then raced in blue. White pin lights on either side defined a travel lane, and coordinates appeared on an overly revealing that the lights were also speed and navigation indicators. The faster she went, the more lights appeared.

'Look at you go!' Bryll encouraged.

'This is fun!'

Help completed training mode by demonstrating the various overlays that showed information on levels, quests, rewards, boosts, and bonuses.

With the training done, dark space re-emerged with the flashing diamond that now read *Play*.

On the controller, Shellany pressed buttons and turned dials. 'Now for the fun part. You're going to love constructing your Universe,' she enthused.

'No doubt, but it will have to wait until tomorrow,' Gelda replied with a yawn and a stretch.

'You're going to bed? No!' Hazzy protested.

'It's been a long day.'

'You sure?' said Shellany. 'The construction stage doesn't take that long.'

'How long?'

Shellany thought about it. 'About three hours.'

'Three hours!' Gelda exclaimed.

'That's just an estimate.'

'It only took me an hour to finish construction on my Thalverse,' said Bryll.

'You're closely guided, and you can even automate some of it, which will speed things up.'

'I appreciate your enthusiasm, really, but I'm not sure I can concentrate much longer.' She stifled a groan of exhaustion.

'Listen, my dearest friend.' Hazzy donned a firm tone. 'It's Barlo's last rebirthday, and we are all here right now. There's a good chance you will never, ever again get the chance to play a game with such an awesome cheer squad.'

'She has a point,' Odgio said with a cheesy grin.

Gelda laughed. 'Never, ever?' she teased.

'What about you just play the first level?' Shellany suggested. 'Design only takes about half an hour at the most. You'll earn your Universe Designer badge and qualify as Novice Cultivator.'

'Novice Cultivator!' Hazzy shook his head in wonder.

'Sounds... farmy.' Odgio laughed.

'Design, then sleep!' Bryll suggested.

Fansy had fallen asleep and snored in agreement, making everyone laugh.

Lacking energy to further protest, all Gelda could muster was a slow breath in and a long breath out while blearily smiling at friends intent on seeing her play. It was three hours past her usual bedtime, and while sleep called loudly, something else called louder. Pushing through her lethargy wasn't an option, so instead she ignored it. This was a special evening. Hosting Barlo's rebirthday brought much-needed joy to her home. Keeping the fun going a while longer was worth the added weariness in a tomorrow that only offered quietness and naps regardless of how many hours of rest she got.

Sleep could wait.

'Okay, I'll play!'

Shellany sighed with what Gelda thought was relief, and she wondered if there was another reason for her being here.

'Is there a problem? You seem tense.'

Shellany let out a breath. 'I'm just really keen to see your Universe built. Construction is when a biosphere is most vulnerable, and yours has been prematurely activated, so it's a relief to know it will be secure. Well, if you decide to finish the stage...' Her eyes widened in expectation.

'Let's just see how things go, shall we?' said Gelda.

TEN

More Than a Bang

Hazzy and Bryll left to find sustenance and came back with trays of leftover party food and a hot jug of freshly brewed jova. The small gathering of sleepy friends ate and drank quietly then Gelda settled into her chair and clicked the flashing *Play* diamond. A pensive orchestration played softly in the background and all eyes went to the black rock on the lounge table when a spectrum of colours lit up the grey squares on the white piece of its powerstation, chasing each other around it. The rock kept its shape but turned transparent. Leaning in to get a good look, the small group of friends murmured in approval.

Soothing and wistful music replaced the pensive orchestration. The beat picked up, and the track became dramatic and upbeat. With the aid of Help explaining, the overlay appeared with three lines of type: *Construction, Adaptation, Unity*. The latter two lines turned grey then disappeared. They were replaced by three lines in smaller type: *Design Universe, Planet Cultivation, Intelligent Life*. Again, the latter two lines disappeared. *Design Universe* grew to dominate the overlay with *Yes, Stop* beneath. Gelda was about to press *Yes* when under it in bold and flashing red letters appeared an alert: *DO NOT SELECT STOP. IF ACCIDENTALLY STOPPED, DO NOT DISCONNECT.* Under that was further information: *Selecting Stop will permanently halt all progress in the biosphere and cause irreparable damage to its lifeforms. This process cannot be stopped or reversed once it has started.*

'I guess I shouldn't press *Stop* then?' Gelda joked solemnly.

With a vigorous shake of her head, Shellany said, 'The Stop option was a command error.' She looked up quickly then added, 'At least that's what I heard. Whenever you see a Stop option, do *not* press it. Stopping a game is the worst thing you could do to an emerging biosphere.'

'What happens when it's stopped?' Hazzy asked the question on all lips.

'The game ends prematurely and the biosphere can be severed.'

'Severed?! Ugh, sounds awful. Don't do that!' Hazzy cried out. 'What does severing *do*?'

'No one in their right mind would ever do it,' Shellany replied. 'Severing is when some fool stops a game then disconnects the preservation chamber from the powerstation. Without a power source, the biosphere can't evolve so it just exists forevermore in whatever state it's at in that moment, and everything inside it dies.'

'What's die?' asked Hazzy.

'Cosmo Dome inhabitants generally don't live endless lives like we do. They expire after getting badly hurt or after one lifetime.'

'Only one life?' Hazzy pondered.

'They don't rebirth?' Gelda wondered, mindful of her own recent dilemma.

'They have really basic healing abilities so can't recover after grave harm,' Shellany explained. 'It's called being mortal.'

'Where do they go when they die?'

'They turn to dust,' Shellany replied.

There were several murmurs of dismay as those present were unable to fathom the concept of mortality.

'I'm having the same issue with my microworlds,' said Barlo. 'They rarely survive past a century.'

Bryll shook his head. 'Gone like pickings left too long in a bowl. Imagine!'

'Sounds awful!' said Odgio.

'Imagine only having one life!' said Hazzy.

'Barely around for a glimpse of time!' Gelda remarked. 'You would want to make it the best it can be.'

When the murmurs of shock and dismay faded, Gelda very carefully selected *Yes*.

Help spoke instructions supported by additional information on a static overlay just below Gelda's eye level. The first level of Construction was *Design Universe*. Gelda was to play a subquest called Matter Splatter. It was played in remote mode which Help described as a semi-immersive experience. When *Attach Blaster* appeared on the overlay, Gelda inserted the remaining power connector into the powerstation to remotely connect it. *Blaster Enabled* appeared on the overlay with *Initial Splatter: Point and Shoot* underneath. A crosshair appeared out front of the blaster with two gauges below. Each had hollow squares arranged in a semi-circle and an arrow pointing bottom left. One gauge indicated time, the other space.

'Press the trigger, Ma Varda,' encouraged Bryll when Gelda did nothing.

Shellany confirmed with a nod. 'Press it all the way down and point it in the middle of the display. You can't go wrong. Just have fun!'

The blue energy current from the chamber to the blaster's base moved with Gelda as she swung it left and right, getting a feel for it. Steadily, she pressed the trigger until out whooshed a blast of piercing white particles. It was so unexpected that she flinched then laughed, as did the others, but kept the blaster steady and her finger locked in place on the engaged trigger. With rhythmic music keeping the pace, the particles blasted out. They seemed to go on forever before spreading outwards in every direction at varying speeds, casting imagery objects into the air around the small gathering who oohed and aahed until there was no other response left but awed silence.

The particles multiplied and clustered, changing colour, size, shape, and consistency, while the time and space gauges turned from empty to full. Though she made little sense of the moving colours and textures, something told Gelda she was looking at a complex and fascinating living entity. The music turned dreamy as multi-coloured spiralling clouds and twinkling lights emerged against a dark background. Gases and matter swirled and flickered spreading deep into the dark space.

Just as Gelda's finger started to ache and her attention drifted from shooting to discovering what had happened, the particles eased then stopped. The music settled into an ambient hum with mellow beats. She stopped shooting and put the blaster down. The space gauge showed full capacity in solid blue squares while the time gauge still had a few empty slots.

'What did I just do?' Gelda marvelled at the vivid display.

'You populated your Universe.' Shellany's grin was wide and steady.

The empty squares of the time gauge hadn't yet filled when another query appeared. *Organise Universe? Yes, No.*

'This is the fun bit,' said Shellany. 'You get to arrange everything.'

'It's art!' Hazzy murmured.

'Interactive art,' Bryll added.

Pressing *Yes* showed an animated hand that clicked and dragged, pinched and zoomed.

'I get to move things around?' she said just as Help confirmed it. 'What fun!' She stood and clicked on a colourful swirl. *Galaxy 156FR-03* appeared on a popup message. To uplifting music, she moved it away from a thick cluster of objects then zoomed in to find more objects with codenames. Clicking and dragging, pinching and zooming, she arranged planets and stars, dust and dark matter, moons, comets, and gas, tapping her foot to the beat.

'Put something there!' Hazzy pointed at a blank spot.

'That one looks like a car. Oh, and there's a house!'

Bryll laughed. 'That cluster looks like Finkle!' The

arrangement of stars certainly did resemble Gelda's housemate.

With plenty of input from friends, Gelda shuffled and rearranged cosmic objects until her Universe was visually pleasing with a good balance of colours, shapes, and space except for one galaxy. It was in a small group of galaxies towards the edge of a modest supercluster. When she hovered a finger over it, the codename 342MW-11 appeared. Sometime about it bothered her. It just looked out of place, wrong somehow. Even the music seemed to grow a little melancholic as she considered the galaxy. Her concerns grew when it refused to move when she clicked on it. Gelda couldn't put anything near it either, so it remained separated. 'Why is there always something in resistance?' she grumbled.

'Nothing's ever perfect,' said Odgio. 'But just look at what you made!'

He was right. Instead of worrying about it, she focussed on the rest of her newborn Universe biosphere.

'It's so beautiful!' exclaimed Hazzy.

'It's way more epic than my Thalverse!' exclaimed Bryll.

'Is that the cosmo?' Fansy woke and held her almost-empty elixir decanter up to gesture towards it.

'It's a Universe,' Bryll explained.

Gelda sat back in her seat to admire the full effect. Seeing it displayed so magnificently mystified her. She wondered if the display was an honest representation of the Universe biosphere inside the chamber. 'Is it a simulated environment?' she asked Shellany.

'It's a true transmission,' Shellany replied. 'It's also where the main gameplay occurs. What happens here happens for real inside the Universe.'

'Congratulations, Gelda,' said Help as the time gauge showed full capacity in solid yellow squares. 'You have achieved Designer status.' A badge with the word, *Designer*, appeared then the query, *Explore the Universe biosphere? Yes, No.*

'I did it!' Gelda high-fived the others.

Help told her to pick up the steering wheel, then Gelda got to explore her newly designed Universe. With uplifting music enhancing a sense of wonder, mouths fell open and tongues quieted as Gelda navigated her way through the vast darkness of space to an assortment of planets, asteroids, natural satellites, meteoroids, and comets that came gradually into focus. Some grew so large they filled the room or bigger, while others turned from specks to small enough to cup a hand around. The ever-moving display went on and on, deeper into space as though it never ended.

Bryll suggested going to a billowy thing with gases lifting from it that turned out to be a star. Hazzy wanted to see a planet with an ice surface and a molten rocky core. Odgio wanted to see a smoky planet with a thick swirling ring around it. Close up, the dark space beyond it disappeared and was dominated by countless small orbiting particles of dust and ice.

'Unfathomable! How can all those worlds fit inside something the size of a hand ball?' Hazzy marvelled.

'We all think the infinite void beyond Oridian is just there to contain more of our worlds, but what if it comes to an end and there's something else beyond it?' said Odgio.

'Maybe we're someone else's biosphere,' added Bryll.

Hazzy shook her head in wonder. 'Worlds within worlds within worlds.'

Gelda checked the time on the wall clock. 'That took an hour!' With a yawn and a stretch, she stood. 'That's definitely it for me. I'm off to bed.'

'No!' Shellany cried out.

Gelda wondered why she sounded so desperate, but before she could question the odd response, Barlo appeared at the door. 'Sorry, Grandma! I got caught up in conversations.' His eyes instantly went to her new Universe biosphere that shrouded the room in cosmic wonder. 'Is *this* your game? Wow!' Oblivious to anything but the Universe, he wandered further into the lounge room in a random path while inspecting the various cosmic objects, shaking his head in disbelief. 'It's so sophisticated!'

Gelda gave a knowing smile. Raquin had obviously mentioned the game to him in a less than favourable light. 'I've only just finished designing it. Next, I'm required to cultivate the planets – that's what its worlds are called – then develop intelligent life.'

Barlo still shook his head in wonder. 'That's exactly what I do with my microworlds. I can't believe something so old is this complex! He sat on the edge of her seat and smiled at Shellany. 'Tawawa! I'm Barlo!'

'Tawawa, Barlo!' Shellany told him her name.

'Will you keep playing?' he asked his grandma.

'I'm not sure, darling. It's late.' To quell his protests, Gelda showed him the demo mode.

It only made him gush even more. 'Play some more so I can

see it in action,' he pleaded.

His interest prompted Gelda to ask, 'I actually bought it for your rebirthday but didn't think you'd like it. Do you want it?'

Barlo shook his head. 'I love it but, no. You play. It's the perfect hobby for you!'

'She has to, now,' said Shellany. 'It's founded on her DNA.'

'See? It's a sign!'

Overjoyed to have her grandson interested, Gelda considered playing on. It was good to feel needed again, especially when it involved sharing an interest with him. While the others pleaded with her to carry on, she listened with a bemused smile then admitted she had already decided to do so.

Shellany seemed overly relieved. 'Seeding the planets will only take an hour or two,' she said.

'Seeding them? How curious!'

Shellany nodded. 'You'll see. It's pretty cool.'

With lights low, house quiet, and a third cup of steaming jova in front of her, Gelda squeezed her tired eyes a few times and rolled her shoulders then returned her attention to the game. The instructions Help gave on the overlays were enough so she muted the audio, which made it easier to concentrate, and she enjoyed the music much more without the voice layer. After many decanters and a long night, her friends contentedly sipped jova and watched in silence.

The second construction level, Planet Cultivation, was a sub-quest called Seeding & Feeding. *Determining Habitable Planets* and an hourglass appeared on the overlay. A visual list of planets was arranged in galaxies and coloured grey. On a second overlay, hundreds of tiny spacecrafts appeared in rows with the title *Seeding Drones*.

Soft beats remained in the background as *Demo* flashed over-top of the display and the view zoomed in on a dull and lifeless planet. A spherical grid with dots on hundreds of intersecting points surrounded the planet, then one by one, the drones flew down and settled on the points. They flashed green then shot fuzzy balls. Only moments later blues, oranges, yellows, and greens spread across the planet. The drones flashed white then liquid from spouts poured down drenching the planet. The planet transformed some more, then thin pulsing rings appeared around it and the demo ended.

'If I'm to do that for every planet in every galaxy in the entire biosphere it will take days not hours! There must be squillions!' Though Gelda spoke softly, it was with an edge of panic. Sleep seemed a reasonable option.

'It's a cumulative process,' was all Shellany said.

Gelda didn't quite know what she meant but was too tired to question it and instead picked up the steering wheel. When she pressed *Play*, a planet shot to the foreground of the display. Like in the demo, a grid surrounded it. Gelda positioned the drones on its points then *Phase One: Drop Microbes* appeared. To an upbeat track, when the drones flashed green, she pressed the button on the wheel and the fuzzy microbe balls pelted from the circle of drones towards the planet within. A coin meter appeared in the top corner of the display accompanied by clinking sounds. She wondered what if was for but kept shooting.

The level was more fun than the demo had suggested, especially when she realised she could zoom in on a drone. The fuzzy balls its torpedo shot were yellow and green with specks of brown and red in them. They sped towards the planet quivering with life and exploded onto the surface. She couldn't zoom in past the drone but could see that the bland surface soon speckled with colour as the microbe balls splattered far and wide, blending with other splatters, spreading across the planet.

'That's pretty cool,' said Odgio.

Gelda looked up to find that, other than Shellany, he was the only one still awake. Even Barlo snoozed. She gave him a tired smile of appreciation. Odgio had always been supportive of her, which made her wonder why their marriage had failed until she reminded herself that no marriage lasted forever. Friendships, on the other hand, did. Gratitude warmed her heart and encouraged her onwards.

Phase Two: Drop Environmental Conditioner appeared next on the overlay. When she pressed *Shoot!* clear liquid spurted from a spout on each drone.

'Water?' she enquired.

When Shellany didn't answer Gelda turned to find her on her aide again. She had been checking it more than watching Gelda's progress.

Shellany looked up. 'What? Oh, yes. It's water but with life-conditioning chemicals in it.' She went back to her aide.

Her attention back in the quest, Gelda watched the conditioned water quickly and efficiently saturate the planet. Satisfied with the outcome, she read instructions for *Phase Three: Apply Time Stabiliser* to discover that it didn't require any gameplay, only enabling. Thin pulsing rings appeared and continued to pulse as the next planet required her attention.

'Tawawa!' came a whisper from the dark space behind the lounge setting.

Gelda turned to find Raquin smiling at her. 'Tawawa, love.'

Raquin's eyes wandered around the Universe. 'What *is* this?' she exclaimed softly.

Her voice roused Barlo from sleep. 'I thought you'd left without me,' said Barlo.

Raquin laughed. 'I fell asleep on a deck chair. Are you ready to go?'

Barlo shook his head the pointed it towards the sofa. 'Sit down, Ma. You've got to see this.'

Raquin groaned. 'I need sleep and evidently so do you. We leave in less than a day and there's so much to do!'

'What's left? You've already packed.'

'Mostly, but you haven't.'

'It'll take me a few hours at the most. Sit!'

Raquin surrendered. She squished onto the end of the sofa, returned Gelda's tired smile, then her and Shellany made acquaintances. When she asked what was going on, Barlo caught her up. 'Sounds intriguing. Don't let me stop you, Ma.'

As if on cue, the full coin meter burst. Gelda was about to ask Shellany what it represented when twice as many drones appeared on the overlay as the first time and two planets shot to the foreground of the display. 'Oh, I get it,' she addressed Shellany without taking her attention from the quest. 'I seed one planet, then two, and so on.'

Shellany didn't even look up from her aide but simply nodded. 'Until your entire Universe is cultivated.'

Gelda paused the game. 'Is there a problem?'

'What?'

'You've been on your aide for the past hour or so. Is there something else that needs your attention more than this? You can leave, if you need to.'

'No, no, it's okay. It's all fine.'

It doesn't seem fine, thought Gelda, but it was none of her business, or so she assumed, and hoped so. She ran through the phases on the two planets, then four appeared, and so on. The planets kept multiplying until all habitable planets in the first galaxy were cultivated. 'Aha! This speeds things up!' she said. When next a close up of a galaxy appeared on the display with its habitable planets flashing green, Gelda didn't miss a beat. She just carried on cultivating planet after planet, galaxy after galaxy.

'You're good at this,' Raquin observed.

'There's nothing to it. It's just running through a process, then repeating it.'

Barlo shook his head. 'Being thorough is underrated.'

'As is perseverance,' said Gelda. Without it she would be much worse off in her own life under the current circumstances. To feel lively again was a grand ambition.

Time crept past midnight. With sleeping friends and enthusiastic family around her, Gelda found renewed energy in wanting to see her Universe made. Galaxy after galaxy thrived under her touch. While repetitive, she found it soothing watching her Universe come to life. With almost the entire Universe cultivated, the final galaxy emerged from the depths of dark space. Planet after planet consented to cultivation until the last.

The drones surrounded it easily enough. The microbes dropped without a hitch, as did the pouring of the Environmental Conditioner and the Time Stabiliser. The whimsical music that had played throughout the level subdued.

With Gelda grumbled and mumbled, Shellany looked up from her aide. 'What's the problem?'

'This last galaxy is taking ages to cultivate.'

'It's the drones,' said Barlo. 'Look. The power bar is at zero.'

Shellany shook her head. 'It's not the drones. Something is causing a lag.'

Just as she said it, the drones stopped firing and cultivation stalled at 93%.

'How far did it fall?' asked Shellany

'When the cat knocked it over? Just the kitchen bench but it rolled away and hit the wall.'

'It's odd that the mailcage didn't protect it.'

'Not really. It was old and fell apart.'

'That would do it.'

Gelda checked what galaxy it was and groaned. 'I suspected as much. It's Galaxy 342MW-11, the same one that refused to move or let me put anything near it in Level One.' She sank back in her armchair and sighed.

Shellany nodded thoughtfully. 'Hm. And the planet?'

Gelda clicked on the planet for its details.

'Codename PEACH,' everyone who was awake said at once.

Suggestions were presented, analysed, and dismissed. Gelda suppressed a desire to call it a night and not be tempted otherwise, but she couldn't sleep until the issue was resolved.

'What about a minigame?' said Bryll, suddenly awake and contributing.

'Yes. That could work.' Shellany got Gelda to go to the Bonuses & Extras menu. 'Scroll down. You want something simple to earn maximum coins with little effort. Yes, there! Tile matching.'

'She's great at those,' said a half-awake Hazzy.

Gelda clicked on the minigame and very efficiently matched tiles of the same colour to clear them from the board. It took playing it three times to earn enough coins for another set of drones. To suspenseful music, everyone sat up in anticipation as she ran through the three planet cultivation phases. It was a tense wait for the Time Stabiliser. The thin rings seemed to pulse forever but then finally *Planet Cultivation Complete* appeared. The suspenseful music ascended into uplifting. One by one, habitable planets were swathed in a swirling blast of light, texture, and colour.

'All your habitable planets are cultivated!'

'Congratulations, Gelda,' said Help as confetti and coins burst from a big bright orange container labelled *Bounty Box*.

It was indeed a relief to finish the level and earn her Cultivator badge.

'Novice Constructor!' Hazzy exclaimed so loudly she almost

woke Fansy.

Exploring the cultivated planets revived everyone's attention. The first planet Gelda chose to explore had a gaseous atmosphere. The planet was abuzz with electromagnetic activity. On the surface, mists rose through mammoth jagged rock mountains while water from up high dug narrow crevices to the base.

'The Universe model is so much more complex than Thalverse,' Bryll remarked.

'All that life with so much potential,' Hazzy mused.

'And inside something so small,' said Odgio.

Gelda took off to the far reaches of her Universe.

'Where are you going now with such determination?' Barlo wanted to know.

'That annoying planet that took all my time.' While there were many intriguing planets to choose from, Gelda was most interested in seeing PEACH in Galaxy 342MW-11.

'Isn't it odd how it's always the problems that take our attention,' Hazzy mused.

'Tell me about it,' replied Gelda. Through the galaxy she cruised, to the solar system with the glitching planet.

As she drew nearer, Bryll said, 'It's just a lump of rock.'

'That massive orange ball beyond it is more interesting,' Raquin remarked.

Shellany looked up from her aide. 'That's a star.'

As Gelda passed through its atmosphere, the stats displayed relatively high levels of oxygen, methane, carbon dioxide, and other gases to support life. Below lay patches of blue, green, and tan. Cruising above the surface showed a verdant oasis teeming with colourful foliage and a vast array of creatures.

'Wow, that's an impressive world!'

Gelda had expected it to be less impressive but was blown away by its beauty.

'All that extra cultivating certainly paid off,' Barlo remarked.

For now, thought Gelda. Something told her it wasn't the last time PEACH would be a cause for concern.

ELEVEN
Play or Pass

When the *Planet Evolution In Progress* bar appeared, Raquin said, 'Okay, now it's definitely time to go.'

'It is,' Barlo conceded.

The pair said goodbye to everyone, then Gelda walked them out.

At the door, Barlo hugged her tightly. 'I'm so happy you've found something meaningful, Grandma. I'd love to see you play some more.'

Raquin's hug was shorter but just as warm. 'Me too, Ma. It's the perfect thing for you right now.'

'Thanks, love. It's hectic but fun.' Gelda laughed. 'I can't believe I'm building a biosphere of mini worlds!'

'You'll do great. Keep us in the loop on your progress.'

'It's a shame you both can't stay longer to see how it all turns out, but you've got a great adventure ahead of you! Are you excited?'

'Very much so!'

After a second round of hugs Gelda said, with a tear in her eye, 'I'm going to miss you both so much, but have a memorable trip!'

'Thanks for an amazing party, Grandma. I love you! Tawawa!'

'Tawawa!'

Waving goodbye to them from the door, Gelda took a moment to breathe in the fresh air and enjoy the silence. It was well past midnight, and the neighbourhood was quiet. Back inside, she considered tidying a little but decided to leave it to the cleaners in the morning. Lights dimmed and doors closed, she returned to the lounge room.

All eyes turned to her.

'We've made an executive decision,' Bryll announced with arms folded over chest in a defiant gesture. 'We're not going home until you finish building your Universe.'

Hazzy shrugged. 'We figured you might as well. It's already way past your bedtime,' she pointed out.

Odgio nodded. 'Imagine waking up to a Universe biosphere that you built yourself!'

'Yes, how good would that be!' Hazzy sought parallel enthusiasm from those around her. From within an elixir stupor beside her, Fansy mumbled. 'Even Fansy agrees!'

Everyone laughed.

'*And* you'll be a third of the way into the game,' Bryll pointed out.

'Kind of,' said Shellany. 'Adaptation is almost twice the length of Construction, and there's no telling how long Unity will take.'

'What happens after the game ends?' asked Hazzy.

'It doesn't really end. You continue to monitor it and intervene when something goes wrong, or if your Universe steers off-course with its evolution – which can sometimes happen, especially when they grow complex.'

As they talked, Gelda sipped her fifth jova and took a bit of a puffly. When they waited for her reply, she simply smiled and said, 'I'd already decided to keep playing.'

Hazzy harumphed dramatically. 'Why didn't you say?!'

'I couldn't get a word in,' Gelda teased. It was quite odd that she suddenly felt rather good. It was as though her energy levels had flipped or been given a magical boost – or perhaps mind and body had simply succumbed to the notion of no sleep and reluctantly gave all they had. Whatever the reason, she was simply glad for the zest to continue. 'Let's get to it then, shall we?'

To soft dramatic music, the progress bar filled with green and *Planet evolution complete* appeared underneath. Five animated gold stars bounced onto the main overlay then the message, *Your DNA has fostered excellent diversity in the Universe. It now supports advanced and complex species that have evolved in many and varied ways and possess maximum potential for eternal evolution.*

'Five stars is the most you can earn, and look, you've earned maximum bonuses!' Shellany pointed to an animated gold ribbon in the top left.

'Congratulations!' said everyone.

As rows of simple organisms appeared in the foreground, Gelda said to her Universe, 'Yet. Let's see what you've got.' With Help's audio still muted, she read: '*On 89% of habitable planets in Universe, microbes have evolved into multi-cellular organisms. It is now your task to steer their evolution until they are sophisticated beings that think and feel.*'

Passing level three would complete the first of three stages of the game and she would earn the Creator badge.

What a night this has turned out to be! thought Gelda as she pressed *Yes* to confirm play.

Phase One was called *Merge to Evolve*. It involved playing a subquest called *Start the Smart* where the aim was to merge species to create sentient and sapient beings.

'I love merge games!' exclaimed Bryll.

On the overlay, a game board appeared with rows of species pre-selected by the game system. They were based on planet cultivation results from the previous level.

'Aw, look at those cute little critters!' Hazzy pointed at the organisms tumbling in their rows on the display.

'They all look the same,' was Odgio's opinion.

It was true that at first glance they were difficult to tell apart, but closer inspection revealed subtle differences. As Gelda merged the organisms in sets of three or more, new and more complex organisms were created. Their differences grew more distinct as bacteria, plants, and other things without skeletons morphed into more physically complex things that could float, swim, climb, fly, and walk.

'You're getting the hang of it fast,' Shellany observed.

'She's a natural,' Hazzy agreed.

'Almost like it was made for her,' said Bryll.

Fansy woke with a cough and a groan. 'Where am I? What's happening?' She stretched and sat up. 'How long was I asleep?'

'A few hours,' Bryll told her, distractedly.

'And you're still playing?'

No one bothered answering.

She grumbled something about the bathroom then staggered out.

The happy music reflected the joys of satisfying play. The coin meter filled, the bounty box overflowed, bonuses were awarded. By the end of the level, the simple cellular organisms became beings with hair, eyes, arms and legs, wings, and brains sophisticated enough to process and understand, and that possessed the fundamental skills needed to survive inside the emerging Universe biosphere.

'I've played a lot of games in my times, but this one is extraordinary,' Odgio remarked.

The game system returned each species to its origin planet then *Assigning Primes* appeared with a progress bar.

'This is a critical point in construction,' said Shellany. 'The game system determines what is the most advanced civilisation in each galaxy then designates its planet as the galactic prime, which means it becomes the foundation civilisation for every other cultivated planet in its galaxy.' She wore a serious expression when she looked up. 'This is probably the biggest turning point in the whole game. The Primes of your Universe determine its intelligence and whether it survives for always, for a long time, or for barely a glimpse of the eternal timeline.'

A long silence followed as everyone soaked up the magnitude of it all.

'It might not survive?' Gelda asked in barely a whisper.

'Maybe, maybe not, but it will hold on for as long as it can. It will even struggle if it has to.'

'How awful!' said Hazzy.

While the game system assigned the prime planets, Gelda sat back and closed her eyes, grateful for a break from concentrating, but the oohs and aahs of her friends had her opening them again. On the display, a galaxy zoomed to the foreground. Its habitable planets took turns being the centre of attention until one remained with *Prime* above it, then another galaxy took its place and the process repeated itself. To the side was a time scale gauge coloured in a gradient band from red to green. It indicated how long the Universe would survive. On one side in red was the fleeting timespan of an *Age*, followed by *Epoch*, *Period*, *Era*, *Eon*, and *Icod*. On the other side in green was the maximum timespan a Cosmo Dome player could accomplish for their biosphere, *Eternity*.

As primes were assigned, the arrow lifted into Epoch and crawled slowly towards Period.

'I can't look.' Hazzy turned away.

Bryll did the same, but the others watched on. As the galaxies were assigned suitable primes and the arrow crept to *Era*, Shellany got up to stretch her legs, inspiring Gelda to do the same.

Fansy returned from the bathroom. 'Whoa, you could cut the tension in here. All so serious over a game.'

'It's *way* more than just a game,' said Odgio.

With a soft chuckle, Fansy squeezed back on the sofa and closed her eyes. 'More than a game.' She chuckled awhile then fell into a snooze scattered with mumbles and snores.

With only a few galaxies left, the arrow on the gauge reached the Era segment then tipped into Eon.

'It's almost in the green!' Odgio softly exclaimed as the arrow reached Icod.

With two galaxies to go, Hazzy pried open an eye to see the arrow almost reach Eternity.

'Eternity!' Odgio cried out as the arrow reached the farthest side of the gauge and applauded.

'No, Icod. Um, Eon.' Shellany informed a second later. With one galaxy to go, the arrow fell.

'Era,' Gelda noted as it fell more. 'What's going on?'

'I bet it's that pesky planet again,' said Bryll.

'Shh! You'll jinx it!' Hazzy cautioned, but it was too late.

The *Assigning Primes* progress bar stopped moving and flashed red. Below it in small red type: *151-34/36 Error.*

'That's not good,' Hazzy remarked.

They all looked to Shellany who shook her head and frowned.

'I should have known we'd run into problems. Universe is notoriously glitchy.'

'What? Why didn't you say?' Gelda was a little miffed that she didn't know sooner. She unmuted Help who very pleasantly recited the same message on repeat, 'To ensure overall sustainability of your Universe biosphere, please select a suitable prime planet for this galaxy.'

'Help's no help.' A quiet chuckle escaped Odgio at his unintentional choice of words.

Gelda clicked on the galaxy's info icon. '342MW-11. It's the same one as before.' No one said anything, even when she opened its data and viewed its planets. PEACH flashed red. Its stats revealed its evolution had stalled at 48%.

'No!' cried Hazzy.

'48%?! It's supposed to be the most advanced civilisation in its galaxy,' Shellany grumbled. 'I should have known it would glitch!'

'How would you know?' Gelda wondered, but Shellany only shook her head.

'What a shame!' Bryll sighed. 'And you were so close to earning your Constructor badge, Ma Varda.'

Gelda scrolled through the data of the problematic galaxy. 'This is weird. All of its potential primes are dulled out, but the planet codename PAACU is at 96% suitability.' She brought PAACU to the foreground, and they admired its progress. The flora and fauna were well balanced and diverse, and its stylish societies had many functional structures and technological advancements.

Gelda clicked on its history to see hamlets turn to villages then develop into towns and cities, while its people became smarter and more sophisticated. In awe, she watched people hunt and forage, build homes, invent tools and machinery. Families shared meals, children played, communities grew.

'Imagine not knowing you're inside a tiny dome being controlled by someone playing a game!' mused Odgio.

'Someone so big, you can't even see them,' Shellany pointed out.

'Unfathomable!'

'But it's lovely!' said Hazzy, the eternal optimist.

'It's indeed similar to Leffon,' Bryll noted. 'They're quite advanced, too.'

'It really does have a pleasant vibe,' Gelda agreed.

'I'd live there,' Bryll decided.

The PAACU stats revealed that its advanced civilisation used sense and reasoning, symbols and language, and were capable of creating complex social structures. What Gelda found most encouraging was the balance between the natural environment and what the planet's people made to keep them progressing and fulfilled.

'It's almost perfect. Why wouldn't the game system choose it instead?'

'I'd say PEACH is supposed to be the prime, but something went wrong,' said Shellany.

'Again,' said Hazzy.

'So something stopped it from evolving,' Bryll suggested.

'A certain cat who likes to paw things off counters,' grumbled Gelda. She slumped back in her armchair, her miraculous energy boost now depleted by yet another failure.

Shellany studied the data for a while then thought for a moment. 'It could be a civilisation error or a time stabiliser issue.'

Gelda waited for her to say more, but Shellany stared off into the middle distance for a moment then returned her attention to her aide. It was all the encouragement Gelda needed to decide it was time to call it a night. 'That's it then.' She hoisted herself out of the armchair.

'You're giving up?' Hazzy enquired.

'I'll finish in the morning.' Gelda looked around while figuring out the least amount of tidying and switching of things off to do before she could sleep.

Bryll stood with a shake of his head. 'I don't know, Ma Varda. Maybe it's too broken to play.'

'You tried your best,' Odgio acknowledged as he also got to his feet.

'As much as I hate to say so, it does seem like a lost cause,' said Hazzy, joining them.

Everyone grumbled and mumbled in defeat until Shellany sprang to her feet. 'No!' she blurted in a contrary manner to her previously soft-spoken tones.

Everyone except Gelda sat down again, sending worried glances her way.

Upon seeing their reactions, Shellany turned her head away then leaned in to Gelda and whispered, 'Can we talk somewhere private?'

Trying not to worry, Gelda nodded and led Shellany outside where there was no one around. They stood near the pool.

'What is it?'

With obvious reluctance, Shellany said, 'Your Universe is in danger.'

'What do you mean?'

'I didn't want to say anything – I didn't want to panic you or influence your gameplay experience – but someone's after it.'

'A thief? Why? Who?'

Shellany drew in a deep breath. 'A Gorgon collector.'

'A *Gorgon*?!'

'Yes, which is why you need to finish construction.'

Gelda frowned. 'What difference does that make?'

'Once it's built, they won't want it.' Gelda's confused expression prompted Shellany to explain, 'It's pretty messed up, but collectors sever biospheres from their preservation chambers so that they stop evolving.'

'That is messed up. Why?'

'They're worth more when they're suspended in time. In some worlds severed Cosmo Dome biospheres pass as art.'

'In Gorgon worlds, you mean?'

'Yes.'

'How do you know all this?'

'An inside source,' Shellany said quietly.

Gelda gazed absently at the rippling light patterns on the water. Her head reeled. She tried to arrange the many questions that tumbled in her mind, not least of which was Shellany's true identity, then decided on, 'Why do I get the feeling you're not telling me everything?'

'I'm not,' Shellany confessed. 'But I promise to answer all of your questions after you've finished construction. I'm not bribing you, it's just—'

'They're coming, aren't they? The thief?'

After a brief hesitation, Shellany nodded. 'I'm not sure when.'

'Here? To my house?'

Another forlorn nod.

Gelda located the nearest deckchair and fell back on it. She closed her eyes and let out a long breath.

Both were quiet for a moment, then Shellany said quietly, 'We can save your Universe, Gelda. Severing can only happen during construction, then once it's built, the biosphere fuses with the preservation chamber and it's protected forevermore. Now you see why it's really important that you finish construction tonight?' Shellany sat on the chair next to her. 'May I ask a personal question?'

'Go ahead.' Gelda didn't bother opening her eyes.

'How many years past rebirthing are you?'

Gelda couldn't stop from laughing. 'Is it that obvious? Almost a century,' she confessed.

'What's stopping you?'

'I wish I knew. Nothing. Everything.'

'Hm. Are you ancient?'

'Yes, but...' She trailed off into nowhere then asked, 'Why?'

'It happened to me a few lifetimes ago. Apparently, it's happening to us ancients more and more these days.'

'*You're* ancient? You're so vibrant and dynamic, I thought you were on your first life! Your last rebirth must have been quite something.'

Shellany gave a short laugh. 'There's rebirthing and there's re*birthing*. Cosmo Dome will help.'

'How can playing a game help?'

'It has this unspeakably profound, almost cathartic, effect on players and Universe is more mind-blowing than all the other models combined. You'll see for yourself if you keep playing. Will you?'

'It doesn't seem like I have a choice. If I don't, then it won't survive.'

Shellany lay back, too. 'I'm sorry, really. I honestly didn't want to put pressure on you. Cosmo Dome is meant to be played for pleasure, but once it's built you can do exactly that, and believe me when I say it's worth it.'

'You've played it?'

Shellany sat up and looked over at Gelda with a nod and a

smile. 'I have so much to tell you, Gelda, but first, your Universe needs you. Coming?' She held out a hand.

Gelda hesitated and asked herself, *If I'd known that playing Cosmo Dome would lead me here, would I still play?* The answer surprised her. She took the hand Shellany offered and together they returned to the lounge room.

All eyes were on them when they walked back inside. They had stopped by the kitchen and gathered up leftover desserts and more jova.

'Leave if you wish, but the game will go on,' Gelda said before anyone could steer her off the mission to save her Universe.

Hazzy frowned and raised her brows several times.

'You're going to keep playing?' Odgio shook his head in disbelief.

'Everything deserves to live, even something with a limited lifespan,' was all Gelda said.

'Then I guess we need more jova,' said Bryll and offered cups all around.

Fansy laughed. 'What a night!'

TWELVE
Befuddled

While they drank and ate, Shellany studied the data for PEACH in Galaxy 342MW-11 then reached into a backpack and pulled out a codeboard.

'Oh, so you're a programmer!' said Bryll. 'That explains how you know so much about the game.'

Shellany simply nodded and smiled as she connected the codeboard to the mainframe via the unused port. When everyone wondered how she got past the game's security, she said, 'I used to work on a system just like this.'

'That's useful. And timely. Are you going to reprogram the planet?'

'I wish. It doesn't work like that. There are rules. Everything has to be a part of the game.' Rows of data moved and changed as she tapped away. 'This is just an interim fix,' she explained as she clicked. 'If I had my full setup and more time I'd be able to do more than just add a workaround. I've added a loop-hole to pause the time stabiliser long enough to accelerate its prime civilisation.' She clicked more keys then exited the data field.

The Universe biosphere filled the display again, and all heads turned to marvel at the cosmic wonders around them. In the foreground PEACH dominated the view. Vast deep oceans dominated few landmasses that were green and tan with the occasional white patch.

'Pretty,' Gelda remarked and everyone murmured in agreement.

Shellany got Gelda to click the Events icon on the main overlay. Now, first on the list, was a new roughly drawn icon for a sidequest called Pair with Flair. When Gelda clicked it, an unrefined game sample played. Stick figures wandered around a primitive village, some with coloured blocks above their heads.

'Sorry about the draft quality, but you get the idea.'

'A matching game?' Hazzy wondered.

Shellany nodded. 'It's fast-paced, limited time. The aim is to match compatible couples to generate intelligent offspring.'

'Seems simple enough,' said Odgio. 'You just match the coloured blocks.'

Hazzy squinted her eyes. 'But they're all kind of a reddish-brown.'

'Look closer. They've all got different hues,' Gelda pointed out but agreed that it required a discerning eye. Some were quite similar.

'Just keep focused and you'll do great,' Bryll encouraged.

'I've made the sidequest playable in semi-immersive mode so

you can zoom in on each society,' said Shellany.

Shellany ran through sidequest strategies. Before starting to play, Gelda adjusted the steering wheel then traversed the globe to get a good look at the place from the same height as its flying creatures. From large to tiny, every society on PEACH was primitive. Scattered villages with crude huts made of stone, straw, and clay were surrounded by land cleared to grow crops and raise livestock. In more populated areas, wheeled carts rolled on dusty roads. PEACH had a long way to go to earn its place as galactic prime.

It definitely seems like something has stopped it from reaching its potential, thought Gelda. She zoomed in on the first society. It was a small village near a forest.

'They look like us!' Bryll exclaimed.

Fansy opened an eye and laughed. 'If we were filthy and lived like Gorgons. Forget this rubbishy place. That other world was much better.'

'She can't just forget it,' Hazzy pointed out.

'I would.' Fansy wasn't paying enough attention to understand the rules of the game. A young soul at the end of an early life, she still bore a carefree attitude.

'They do look remarkably like us though,' said Gelda.

The people of PEACH were anatomically similar to Leffels with upright bodies, legs with feet, and arms with hands. The data showed that they possessed highly developed brains and a strong capacity for speech, reasoning, and creating complex social structures. Their potential for demonstrating behavioural modernity and advancement was defined as excellent, but at their present stage of stunted evolution, they wore animal hides and used basic tools and didn't seem all that capable of solving problems.

Gelda sighed. 'They're so far behind PAACU.'

'Life on PEACH is hard and short,' said Shellany.

'For now. It's time to make things better for them.' Gelda pressed *Play*. A countdown appeared. 'Three... two... one... *Go!*' Everyone read the numbers on the overlay. A timer on the upper left started at five minutes. Since the new sidequest wasn't incorporated into the full game system there was no soundtrack.

Gelda started at a village by a river. Tapping one nominated person highlighted them. Tapping a second person coupled them with the first. If they matched, the floating boxes above their heads turned purple. A wrong choice would only waste time, so Gelda made sure to choose wisely. With help from everyone, she checked and double-checked the hue between the couples with the most potential and who were keen to breed. She made a few mistakes with close hues but soon got the hang of it and found a good rhythm and flow. When the breeding couples in the village were all matched, a progress bar appeared above it that quickly filled and revealed three purple stars. The village transformed into a refined town. Its people started to wear proper clothes and shoes, made more sophisticated tools, and refined their farming methods.

As huts turned to houses, and stone tools to metal, Gelda went to the next society and did the same, and so on.

'There's the other one!' said Hazzy when a single couple stalled a town from evolving.

'You missed a village!' Odgio pointed out a place they'd overlooked.

Travelling from place-to-place Gelda matched couple after

couple, leaving each society advancing until purple stars appeared above it on the overlay.

'Ten seconds to go!' Shellany alerted with one town to go. 'Nine... Eight...'

Bryll sat on the edge of his seat, hitting his thigh with his fingers.

Gelda tapped so fast her fingers turned numb. With ten seconds left and three couples to go, she fumbled and dropped the wheel.

'Three... two... one...' read the timer, then, '*Game Over.*'

The *Wah-wah* fail effect sounded as the extra game stream vanished and System kicked back in.

Gelda fell back in her seat, the wheel still in her hand.

Help's icon went from dulled-out to green and the voice spoke the words on the overlay, '*You Lost a Life.*'

'What does that mean?'

Shellany cupped her head in her hands and grumbled to herself. Looking up, she let out a loaded sigh. 'If you fail a level, you lose a life. I should have explained. Sorry.'

'Like in the biosphere?' asked Odgio.

'I *die*?!'

'Yes, but you have two left. Then you have to wait a century before you can play again. We don't have time for that, so be extra careful.'

'Be careful?! Why does it feel like I'm always learning new

and important things in this game without prior warning?' Gelda blurted before remembering the circumstances. A few deep breaths brought enough calm to consider her options.

After Gelda played the roughly made matching game, PEACH's civilised people advanced to 78% and the time scale gauge was back up to Icod, but it still wasn't enough for PEACH to qualify as prime. In tired voices the small group discussed their options. In her favour, Gelda had maximum coins and the bounty box was full of bonuses.

'Did you earn a Divine Intervention charm? Three?! You're really good at this!' Shellany pointed at a 3D head with a halo around it that had the letters DIM above it. 'It gives me an idea!' With everyone waiting for her to finish whatever thoughts stirred, she paced and sat, paced and sat. 'Okay, Plan B. You also have an evolution accelerator that you didn't use in level one. You can go to PEACH in immersive mode and blast the entire planet. It's risky as it can mess with the galactic timeline. But you also have an undo charm, which you don't want to use except in an emergency, but this would definitely qualify.'

Gelda got everything set up then slipped the visor over her head. It fit automatically into place. In divine intervention mode, the display still had game data overlaying the Universe but without the room bordering it. She had an immediate sense of being in the Universe, rather than watching from the outside. She connected the blaster gun and positioned her hands.

'To switch between immersive and remote play tap the right side of the visor,' Shellany told her.

Tapping the visor made the room reappear. Everyone smiled reassuringly. The sole view of the biosphere returned when she tapped the visor a second time.

'There's a test button on the bottom left of the blaster. Use it on a town or city. If it results in instant changes then the accelerator substance works. If not, we'll need a Plan C. To turn the music on or off click the button between your eyes.'

'Definitely on,' said Gelda. Having a soundtrack as guidance made all the difference. She clicked the button and fantastical music began. She adjusted the volume and off she went.

With direction steered by thoughts, she located PEACH ahead, and her attention led her towards it. Gelda had been to many worlds during her lives but travelling to PEACH in immersive mode was a journey like no other. Her raised hand holding the blaster seemed out of place and surreal against a backdrop of space and the planet looming large ahead. Cruising the cosmos through dark space past galaxies, stars, nebulae, dust clouds, black holes, dark matter, asteroids, comets, and meteoroids, was an experience like no other.

'I made this!' she marvelled. 'All of this came from me! It's extraordinary!' She would never again doubt her abilities.

As PEACH drew clearer, she noticed a shard of darkness piercing the blue tint of its atmosphere. A small tremor made her tremble. The music turned somewhat eerie.

'What's that?' she asked Shellany, but when she tapped the visor to exit immersive mode the shard vanished. She described what she saw, but Shellany had no explanation for it, so she pushed it from her mind. The Universe contained many phenomena that were unfamiliar to her; it was probably nothing to worry about.

With the music a touch dramatic, Gelda entered PEACH's atmosphere easily enough and descended to the lower sky. The black shard reached down to the planet. Gelda descended to see that it had made a thin, deep hole in an empty region of a large expanse of land.

'Are you seeing this?' she asked.

'No, what?' Her friends only saw PEACH hovering in space on the display, not close-up and engaging like she did.

She tapped the visor to exit and described what she experienced. 'It seems ominous. It's making the Universe tremble. Even the music is a bit worrying. The hole looks deep.'

'What if it's the crack?' said Bryll.

'I think we can agree the fall caused all of this,' said Odgio.

'No, I mean for real. Maybe the hole is the crack?'

'Causing PEACH to glitch...' Shellany cursed then hurried out of the room. She came immediately came back and said, 'Get in there and blast the planet then get out.'

After a quick orbit of the planet, she descended to sky level and soared across the land. She wanted to inspect the hole closer but also to see the people up close before blasting them with a life-altering substance. She headed for a populated area on the same landmass as the hole and aimed down to a walled city where scruffy vendors traded food and wares in ramshackle markets, and sentries guarded fortresses with crude weapons. It was a good city for the test blast. She pressed the button on the blaster. A small ring of pulsing energy propelled from the blaster towards the city. She felt the whoosh of time speeding up as the city grew and changed. The low squat buildings became multi-storeyed apartment and office buildings. The dusty roads with wheeled carts became highways packed with fuelled automobiles.

She exited divine intervention mode and told her friends of the results, then indicated the city by pointing it out on the map overlay.

'Excellent work!' praised Shellany.

'Time to finish the job.' Gelda returned to PEACH.

High above the planet in its outer atmosphere with a good view, she aimed the blaster. Before pressing the trigger, she glanced across to the dark shard not too far away that cut a sharp path down through the sky. The tremor returned stronger than before; the beat of the music increased. Her best chance of fixing the glitch was at its source.

She glided over there. It was darker and more menacing than it had appeared from a distance. 'That cat has some power,' she remarked, missing her sweet little boy.

Hovering just outside of the shard, Gelda pointed the blaster down at the planet. 'Here goes...' She pressed the trigger.

The dramatic beats in the soundtrack increased as rings of the evolution accelerator substance burst out in all directions. She barely had time to be impressed before another tremor happened. The sky rumbled. She glanced sideways just as the substance impacted with the shard. There was an almighty *boom!* followed by a whoosh of energy that propelled her backwards, and then she fell.

Down, to the planet she tumbled. Below, the hole rose to meet her.

'Take me away from the hole!' she repeated over and over, remembering that navigation was thought-directed but also forgetting she could simply tap the visor to exit. The closer she got, the more the hole seemed to grow wider and deeper.

'Take me home!' she cried desperately. A push, or it might have been a pull, wrenched her sideways towards a coastal town. Down to a street and into a room in a house where she found herself sitting in an armchair playing a game, surrounded by friends.

THIRTEEN
Not Even Tawawa

Wah-wah, the fail sound mocked.

'Game Over,' said Help. 'You lost your second life, Gelda. You have one remaining.'

Caught in a whirlwind of severe dizziness, Gelda didn't dare open her eyes for fear she would pass out, vomit, or both.

A high frequency alarm blared.

'Gorgons!' Shellany blurted.

'*Gorgons*?' came many shocked replies.

Gelda peeked out from under a heavy eyelid to see Shellany's aide had a small round alert device attached to it that flashed red and emitted the ear-piercing alarm. Opening both eyes made the room sway then steady somewhat. An attempt to push through the dizziness and nausea only made it worse.

Shellany switched off the alarm and abruptly stood. Her wide eyes flashed to the door, to the display and its equipment.

'Gelda!' She said with authority leaning over the armchair. 'You need to pause the game so we can hide it!'

'Why did you say Gorgons?' Bryll worried.

'Because they'll be here any moment!'

'Why are Gorgons coming here?'

'They want the Universe! Help me get her up. We need her to pause the game so we can disconnect the pieces and hide it.'

Together they helped Gelda sit up and encouraged her to press the pause button on the bottom left of the display.

Hazzy grabbed Gelda's hand and pried her finger from a clenched fist then pushed it against the button.

'That won't work. It has to be intentional. Gelda! Can you hear me? Press the pause button!'

'Pause?' Uncertainty clouded Gelda's focus. 'Am I inside or out?'

'You're out!' Shellany told her. 'Press the button, Gelda. You need to pause it!'

'Pause it,' said Gelda. The moment her finger touched the button, the dizziness vanished and focus returned. 'I'm out,' she muttered. *I saw myself. I was in my house with my friends, playing the game!*

A car screeched to a halt outside.

'They're here! Where's the capsule?!'

Everyone hurriedly searched the table and floor as doors slammed and gruff voices sounded from outside. Gelda somehow made it to her knees to pat the floor. She found the capsule under the table and dropped it next to the working components. Shellany quickly and efficiently disassembled everything. The transmission display vanished from the air and Help stopped blaring warnings. With the equipment put away, the green, blue, and yellow balls looked just as they did before playing.

A loud and near *thump!* made the floor tremble. Stomping feet grew louder by the second. Odgio hurried to the lounge room door and slammed it shut. The others dragged the sofa over and wedged it across.

'The Cosmo Dome!' Gelda stared at it on the table. Inside the preservation chamber, galaxies swirled in dark space. A faint metallic scent wafted from the Universe accompanied by a slight humming sound. She picked it up in one hand and the remaining ball container in the other. It no longer flashed black, white and red but was clear. She was all too aware that separating the chamber from the powerstation now that the game was in progress would mean ending the game and all the life that had so far grown inside the biosphere. 'It won't fit.'

Shellany hurried to her side. 'Try it. Some things aren't what they seem.'

To the sound of the door being bashed from the other side, Gelda dropped the Cosmo Dome carefully inside the clear ball. It fit perfectly. The ball turned black. She placed it inside the capsule and shut the clasp.

As the door opened and the sofa wedged across it was pushed aside, Gelda shoved the capsule under the armchair cushion. Everyone in the room froze as seven foreigners at least twice the size of everyone present stormed towards them.

The first four wore dark red uniforms that matched their skin tones and gave an intimidating bearing emphasised by their bulk. Tarnished metal badges on their caps read, *SHARP, BRISK, FIERCE,* and *FORCE.* They pointed large guns with pulses of dark purple light that zapped and sizzled. The other three wore tight-fitting black uniforms and boots and carried no obvious weapons. The badges on their caps were shinier as if reflecting their status and read, *Commander, Deputy Commander,* and *Captain.*

Gelda's eyes went to the Gorgon wearing the Commander badge. He was the only one who hadn't shaved his head or face. It made him stand out and somehow gave him an outsider's look that drew her to him. While his appearance revealed an obvious Gorgon lineage – large square head, dark purple-speckled eyes, burly and towering frame – a quiet demeanour seemed at odds with the rest of him.

She didn't mean to catch his eye, but when it happened, she experienced a sense of relatability and understanding that she never expected to feel for someone outside of her own people. While she had no idea what to do about it, Gelda held his gaze but didn't get the chance to investigate the odd feeling.

Just then, the black-clad Gorgon with the meanest face and the *Captain* badge, pushed ahead of the others and waved his gun around at them. 'Everyone, up!' he bellowed in a surprisingly high-pitched voice. 'Arms behind your heads, move to the wall. Slowly! Talk, and you lose your tongue!'

SHARP, BRISK, FIERCE, and FORCE provided encouragement by way of weapons pointed in their faces. Gelda looked to Shellany for a sign that they should defend themselves and the coveted game, but her new friend simply gave a minor shake of her head with eyes that said, *'Don't!'*

FOURTEEN
Soft Looking Thing

Ludor took in the scene. It was late for Leffels to still be awake, and the cheerful decorations suggested a recent celebration. It was all hideously vibrant. He watched on as the trievers attempted to bully the Leffels into moving. The firearms they waved around were standard issue weapons, badly made in Gorgon factories, that stopped working after a few brawls. To most off-world people, they looked hi tech and menacing and did the job of subduing rather well. Tonight, on this job of jobs, the Leffels seemed intimidated but not enough to move.

'What are you waiting for?' Captain bellowed.

'Which wall?' a Leffel in a gold pantsuit enquired.

'I don't know!' Captain snarled and looked around. 'That one.' He pointed at the wall near the window, furthest from the door.

The Leffels got up and shuffled there with their hands on their heads.

'You, stay,' Ludor told the feeble Leffel who'd stared at him in an odd way.

She held his gaze belligerently. 'I do have a name, you know. It's Gelda.'

Without bothering to acknowledge her response, Ludor's eyes moved on and settled on a Leffon with a green streak in her hair. 'And you,' he said.

'Shellany,' Gelda informed him.

Ludor turned long enough to scowl at Gelda then addressed Debrov. 'Search her.'

'I don't have it,' Shellany said plainly.

Debrov skulked towards Shellany. Even for a Gorgon she was large, and the Leffon was rather slender, so the difference between them was pronounced, like a toddler next to an adult. 'Hand over the farking toy.' When Shellany didn't respond, Debrov flicked a finger at her chest. Shellany fell fast as though struck hard. 'When Commander commands, you do what he says. Where is it?'

Holding his gaze on her, Shellany stood and remained silent. Ludor held her eyes for a moment then said, 'Trievers, search the place – but no trashing until I give the word.'

The Leffels cried out in protest as everything that could be picked up, examined, and tossed aside was. Just before FORCE tipped over Gelda's Fancy Beings cabinet, BRISK lifted the cushions of the sofa to reveal a capsule. When he shook it, the Leffels gasped, gaining Ludor's attention. Before BRISK tossed it aside, Ludor yanked it from him.

Debrov leaned in close to get a better look. 'It's nothing like the toy.'

'Like you know.'

'I saw the file Boss King sent you,' she confessed smugly.

'You must be blind then. This is just a case.' Ludor pushed her away. He turned the capsule around to locate the clasp and opened it to find three coloured balls and one with moving colours. Consulting his aide, he located the file Boss King provided and compared the real items to the images. They were almost identical. The ball with the moving colours looked just like the toy. While he couldn't be certain if it was built or not, he still held it out with a victorious grin for the squad to see.

'The toy!' Debrov jeered at the Leffels. 'Farkers think you're smarter than us.'

'We could outsmart you four times out of three,' Captain added.

It gained him a chuckle from several Leffels, which in turn earned them a few kicks and punches.

'Enough!' said Ludor. Brawling rarely ended quickly, and he wanted to get the toy back to HQ before dawn and call it a night. He dropped the capsule inside a well-worn pack from his back. 'Let's go.' He headed for the door.

'Don't give it to Boss King. He has no idea what he's destroying!' the green-haired Leffon blurted.

He turned back around.

While Ludor said nothing, Debrov made up for it by getting up in her face. 'Do you even know what we are?' she growled. 'We're Gorgons and we thrive on trashing and bashing! Fark off with your whimpering.' She punched the woman squarely in the stomach. She went down with a groan but wriggled away towards Ludor, reaching for the capsule. Debrov pressed a foot to her back to hold her to the floor. 'I can't decide whether to cut out your tongue or take off your fingers one by one. Maybe both?'

'All of this over a farking toy.' Ludor was getting impatient.

'It's not a toy. It's a biosphere,' the frail Leffon, Gelda, corrected. 'There are plenty of toys around that don't contain living beings. Leave mine alone and go find one.'

He gave her a cursory glance then considered the remaining Leffels. A woman propped up by two others swayed and couldn't keep her eyes open. Ludor guessed she was under the influence of a Leffel stimulant – elixir, if she was lucky enough. He hoisted her up the wall and pressed her against it with hands at her ribs. It instantly woke her up. 'Is it true Leffels can't lie?' he asked casually.

'Yes! No! We can't,' she blurted in confusion. When he eased off the pressure with his hands, she slid to the floor where her knees crumpled beneath her. She glanced remorsefully at the others.

Ludor held the capsule up and addressed them all. 'Tell me now. Is this thing built?'

No one replied. Even after Debrov made threats and the trievers broke more stuff, still they remained silent.

'Look what I found.' Captain appeared at the door swinging a furry critter.

'Finkle!' Gelda cried out. FORCE and BRISK raised their weapons towards her, but she didn't make a move. 'Put the cat down!'

'*That's* a cat?' Ludor had never seen one before. He would've

146

expected something bigger and meaner. The soft-looking thing meowed and hissed and tried to writhe free, but when Captain held it tight, it changed tactics and went limp. Ludor found it curious that while it growled continuously, it didn't fight.

'You don't know what you're dealing with,' said the man in the black suit and red bowtie.

'And he's *black*!' warned the short woman next to Gelda.

'So?' said Captain.

'Black cats have powers.' Everyone turned to stare at Debrov. '...so I've heard.'

When Ludor glanced back at Gelda, she nodded. 'It's true. Cats are unknowable. Best thing you can do is put him down. Gently.'

Ludor had expected more of a sentimental reaction from Leffels and found their blasé reactions disconcerting.

With both hands squeezing the cat's shoulders, Captain held it at eye level. Without blinking or flinching, Finkle stared at him. 'Powers, hey? Let's find out.' Captain released a hand to reposition it around Finkle's throat.

Paw freed, Finkle took the chance to rake claws across Captain's face. Blood trickled in streaks. Captain cursed and let go of the cat. Finkle ran for the door, but Debrov was there waiting. One foot to his head hindered his escape and his life.

Hairs stood up on Ludor's arms. He expected an emotional response from at least one of the Leffels but received nothing but silence. The only Leffel to seem disturbed over the critter's lost life was the green-haired Leffel, Shellany.

'Stop this madness!' she blurted. 'The Universe isn't built, okay? Is that what you want to hear?'

'Shellany – no!' said Gelda.

Ludor noticed her and the Leffel named Odgio share a look.

'I know it's in your nature to destroy things but please do *not* give this to Boss King,' Shellany pleaded.

For his own amusement, Ludor pretended to consider her words. 'Right. I'll be sure to pass on your concerns.' His tone gained chuckles from Debrov and the trievers, and an eye-roll from Captain. *Finally, a break,* he thought as he turned to leave. Thank fark he'd found the toy in time. His release pass was almost in his hands.

'Where the fark did it go?' said Captain.

Ludor turned to see everyone staring at the spot where the cat had been.

'Hims there, then *poof!* Gone,' said SHARP.

'Not quite,' said Odgio quietly.

Ludor detected a change in the air as though something was about to happen that wouldn't work out in his favour. 'Time to go.'

'What about the farkery?' Debrov demanded.

'Now.' Ludor headed for the door.

It surprised them both when Captain vouched for her. 'At least let them trash the place, or they'll be impossible on the drive home.'

'No!' Ludor called back.

'You're being an arsehole,' Debrov called out.

Ludor turned and repeated her own words. 'When Commander commands, you do what he says, right?' The last thing Ludor wanted was to stick around and watch more farkery that achieved nothing more than making more mayhem and wasting his time. 'Gather the trievers. We're leaving.'

Debrov begrudgingly followed him out, but Captain remained. 'Five minutes,' he told the trievers. While he blocked the Leffels in a corner, the trievers trashed the place. FIERCE kicked over the lounge table and snapped off its legs then threw them at a glass mirror. BRISK pulled out a knife and ripped up the sofa. SHARP toppled the cabinet that held the Fancy Beings figurines, sending them into a mass collision, while FORCE yanked down the ornate light fitting and smashed it to pieces.

With their need for chaos briefly satiated, with weapons dangling from sweaty arms, the trievers and their Captain didn't bother looking back at the Leffels as they headed for the door where they were bizarrely prevented from exiting.

'How?' said SHARP.

'What?' said BRISK.

'Fark!' said Captain.

Ignoring them but with a menacing air lingering, Finkle slinked silently from one side of the open door to the other, tail casually swishing. It was almost as if he deliberately pretended not to notice them. When he turned, if he were able to speak, he might have feigned mild surprise, saying something like, 'Oh, it's you.' He calmly sat facing the Gorgons then stretched out his head to rub a cheek against the doorframe while his gaze went to each of them. None of them moved.

'Nothing rebirths that fast,' Captain muttered.

'What now?' asked FIERCE.

'Brace yourselves,' Gelda called out.

The shift from tame to wild was instant. Hissing with claws bared, in a flash, Finkle whooshed around the room, leaving no Gorgon unscathed. It took less than a minute. Blood flowed, limbs flailed, filthy curses were expressed.

On the other side of the door, Ludor and Debrov reappeared to see the squad flailing around the trashed room and the Leffels still huddled in the corner.

'That's all you've got?' Captain bellowed. Leaving a trail of blood, he pushed roughly past Ludor and Debrov, and stormed off after Finkle who was long gone into a place only cats go.

'Trievers!' he called back, forgetting he wasn't in charge of them anymore.

'What the fark did you do?' Debrov demanded of the Leffels.

'Thems do nothing. Was the critter,' FORCE explained walking past to catch up to Captain, followed by the others.

Gelda shrugged. 'He's unpredictable when provoked.'

'We tried to warn them,' said Odgio.

Ludor scowled. He didn't know why he ripped down the last of the decorations – perhaps to get a reaction, or because they were sickeningly lovely.

'Do you feel better now?' Gelda asked.

Ludor grunted and walked out. Enough was enough.

Debrov gave the Leffels a look of disgust. Before she followed Ludor out, she left them with a piece of advice. 'You people really need to find a more worthwhile hobby that playing with a farking toy.'

'It's a biosphere!' the Leffels shouted in unison.

FIFTEEN

Strange Stranger

The moment the Gorgons left, Gelda and guests emerged from the corner where they'd been trapped. They took a moment, each in their own way, to gather their wits.

Gelda wandered around the room surveying the carnage. She absently picked up Finkle's favourite stool – the only thing not broken – and put it back in its place. As she searched for her car keys and valuables, Odgio laughed. Wondering what could possibly be funny under the circumstances, Gelda looked up. As if he'd never left, Finkle sat on his stool, cleaning himself.

'Feel better after your little outburst?' she asked the cat.

Bryll shook his head. 'Those Gorgons have no idea what bothersome times await them.'

'Seven centuries of bad luck might actually be considered a good thing to Gorgons,' Hazzy said.

'Not that it makes a difference to us. They've got my Universe.'

With haste, Gelda navigated her way through broken figurines and furniture and retrieved a set of keys from a drawer in the kitchen. She stepped over the front door that was knocked off its hinges. The others followed her outside. In the street, the Gorgons piled into a long black car. They watched it screech away towards town.

Bryll pointed. 'Uh, there's someone passed out in your yard.'

A wiry man with wild hair roused himself, stumbled to his feet, and proceeded to brush himself down. He wore mismatched clothes and shiny new shoes.

Gelda saw a large disc strapped to his waist, and perhaps her eyes played tricks on her in the low light, but it appeared there were translucent rings pulsating from it. 'Who are you?' Gelda enquired of him. She was pretty certain he hadn't been at the party. Other than Shellany who wasn't an invited guest, everyone else was dressed up, not down.

The man pressed a square button in the middle of the disc. *Shut* flashed in red, and it changed to a steady green *Open*.

As though still dazed, he looked up at Gelda. 'Did they take the Universe?' His eyes scanned everyone for an answer then settled on Shellany. With both mouth and eyes agape, he whispered her name.

Shellany scowled at him then walked right past.

'Where are you going?!' Gelda called out after her.

'I'm sorry!' she called back then ran off down the street.

The man stumbled after her. 'Shellany, come back!' he pleaded, but she was gone.

Parking her curiosity over their connection for the moment,

Gelda headed for her pristine vintage sedan.

'What are you doing?' Hazzy asked

'No one is severing my Universe.'

'You're going after it? Yes. No. Absolutely. We *have* to get it back.'

Bryll caught up with them at the car and blocked the driver's door. 'Are you crazy? They're Gorgons!'

The strange man hurried over next. 'I'm coming too.'

'I don't even know you,' said Gelda.

'I'm Tolbert,' he said absently while holding out the device. It beeped softly and flashed slowly. 'You won't find them without this.'

'Is that a tracking device?' asked Bryll.

'Yes. Set to find the Universe.'

As questions piled on questions in her mind, Gelda took a moment to conduct a lengthy assessment of his demeanour and decided he wasn't dangerous. 'Okay, let's go.'

'And count me in.' Hazzy turned in circles, as though wondering what she needed to take for such a trip.

Gelda, Bryll, Hazzy, and Tolbert got in the car. Gelda started the engine and pulled out into the road just as Odgio appeared at the door, wearing one shoe and fumbling about trying to get his jacket on. 'Wait for me!' he yelled, but he was too late.

SIXTEEN
Meet And Sneak

With Equion's nightfall long since peaked, dawn promised a clear day. For those in the mood for a quiet stroll, there was just enough light to see, yet the streets were still dark enough to remain asleep. They were mostly empty and quiet other than four vehicles on the coastal motorway heading towards the town centre.

The first vehicle was a long black, glossy car with dark windows and eight doors. It was quite a distance ahead of the others and going a fair bit above the local speed limit. The second was a cute little compact town van with bright designs plastered all over it that would have gone faster if it could. Its driver had selected maximum speed, fine when running late for an appointment, but not much help when chasing a fast car on a motorway. The third was Gelda's clean and tidy sedan. And the fourth was the only hovermobile on the electromagnetic rails that ran alongside the mainway.

No traffic meant the hovermobile could choose its speed. It paused just behind Gelda's sedan for a moment before swerving around it and reaching a velocity that made the local limit look like it was for amateurs.

'That's what I need,' said Gelda as it passed. She only drove her sedan a couple of times a week into town. It had a heavy-duty accident buffer and speed stabilisation and was the only thing she owned that hadn't broken yet, which worried her. Inopportune moments seemed to be when things chose to break, and this was the peak of such times.

It was hard enough trying not to think about earlier when she'd found herself in the Universe, especially as she'd been experiencing an odd sensation of being removed from every-thing since returning to what she could only hope was her own familiar world. This wasn't the time to investigate it fur-ther, yet the sensation of being simultaneously connected and disconnected remained. It wouldn't leave, but she could at least push questions aside for now and focus on the more pressing matter of finding the Universe. It was all undoubt-edly bizarre, and yet she hadn't felt this invigorated in many lifetimes.

'There was a town van like that parked at your place,' Hazzy mused from the passenger seat as they reached the colourful van ahead. 'I wonder if it's the same one.'

'Probably one of my guests.' Silently willing the sedan onwards, Gelda shifted from moderate pace to full speed and passed the van.

'We're gaining on them.' Tolbert consulted the tracking device from the seat behind Hazzy.

Gelda glanced in the rearview mirror to see him seated behind her with a lapful of devices. He seemed to be holding a conversation with someone, though next to him Bryll kept his eyes on the road.

For another few kilometres they drove without seeing another vehicle. On the outskirts of town, Tolbert told Gelda to slow down. 'They turned off ahead to the right.'

They all scoured the highway for side roads then saw the bright lights of an eatery ahead.

'In there,' Tolbert confirmed.

Gelda hit the brakes.

'Ooah, I could go a midnight snack,' said Hazzy. 'I've got a hankering for a toasted puffe bredde and maybe a kerai...'

Gelda's stomach rumbled in agreement. Caught up with preparing for and hosting the party, then distracted playing Cosmo Dome most of the night, meant she hadn't eaten much except for snacks during the game.

Bryll raised a brow her way from the seat behind Hazzy. 'Um, in case you forgot, our target is a gang of Gorgons. Maybe hold off on the snacking?'

They turned into the restaurant and parked in the shadows to one side.

'There's that town van again.' Hazzy pointed out the cheerful little vehicle.

'And there's the hovermobile we saw,' said Gelda. 'Should we be worried?'

Bryll shook his head. 'Gorgons don't drive Leffel cars, and this is the only open all-hours restaurant so it's probably just a coincidence.'

'Even so, we shouldn't assume it's not a threat,' said Tolbert.

'Let's focus on one enemy at a time.' Gelda switched off the engine and opened the door.

'What are you doing?' Hazzy cried.

'I'm going to sneak over and look in a window,' Gelda said and attempted to get out.

Hazzy pulled her back in. 'What if they see you?'

Your friend is right,' said Tolbert. 'This isn't the place to confront them. They could have someone watching from their vehicle.'

All eyes went to the long black vehicle parked to the left of the restaurant entrance.

'But this could be our only chance.'

'My guess is their exit strategy will be somewhere private or remote,' said Tolbert.

'That sounds way more dangerous than confronting them in a restaurant,' said Hazzy.

'Which will achieve nothing more than them destroying the place.' Bryll frowned. 'They're not going to just hand it back.'

'No,' agreed Tolbert. 'We have to catch them unawares.'

'That big man pacing about is probably one of them,' said Hazzy, pointing. 'Is that some kind of animal with him?'

All eyes went to the hound who looked up at the triever swinging a bat above its head, toying with his loyalty.

'A dog!' Gelda exclaimed.

'But is it though?' Bryll thought it too large for a house dog and much too playful for a hound dominated by Gorgons. Something was amiss.

'I hope not. Imagine life as a companion animal with a Gorgon as your carer?' Bryll commented.

'It's probably been trained to rip people to shreds,' said Tolbert quietly.

'Poor sweetheart,' Gelda said with a harrowed brow. 'When we get the Universe back, we have to rescue it,' she decided.

'You want to rescue a vicious dog, Ma Varda?' Bryll asked incredulously.

'I think it's a hound,' mused Hazzy.

'It's not the dog's fault. I don't even want to think about it. Let's just wait and see what happens.'

'Good decision.' Bryll was relieved.

'Seems we have a moment to spare. Time for introductions. ' She turned to Tolbert. 'Time for you to explain why you showed up on my doorstep. Who are you and what exactly are you doing here?'

With all eyes on him, Tolbert looked away. The time for this discussion was while the Universe was safe, not while chasing thieving Gorgons. He looked up, his eyes going from one to the other, and confessed, 'I'm Tolbert Shimble.' Taking a deep breath, he added, 'I invented Cosmo Dome.'

Bryll broke the long pause that followed. 'Good gosh! You've been missing for over a century!'

'You have?' Hazzy wondered why.

'You invented Cosmo Dome?' Gelda didn't mean to sound doubting, but it was an incredulous claim. Questions filled her mind, including why he'd reacted to Shellany and vice versa. They clearly knew each other which would explain how she knew so much about the game. Perhaps she worked for him? It was a mystery to solve later.

To catch them up, Tolbert explained everything he knew about the stolen Universe. He logged into System on his aide and showed them statistics on Gelda's Universe and several other Cosmo Domes to prove his point. He paused and looked directly ahead, nodded a few times, then added, 'Boss King has almost completed his set. He's severed one of every model except for the Universe. If we don't get yours back, he'll sever it too, which means all the new life you created tonight will be suspended in time for eternity, never reaching its potential to grow and evolve.'

Gelda watched him fidget and stare ahead of him as though consulting an invisible friend. She considered what he told her then said, 'That is absolutely not going to happen.'

'Agreed,' said Bryll and Hazzy.

'Unfortunately, the end of your Universe biosphere is not the worst of it...' Tolbert said. While reticent to reveal to strangers what was known to only him and SID, his hesitation wasn't meant for effect, though it did achieve that. 'The Universe was the last model I invented, and I only made thirteen of them. A glitch destroyed the other twelve, which means yours is the only one left.'

'What sort of glitch?' said Gelda.

Tolbert was about to reply when Hazzy squealed. 'They're coming!'

The Gorgons exited the restaurant and returned to their large car.

Hand on the ignition button, Gelda waited until they were

on the road then took off after them. They drove for half an hour until the black car pulled up alongside a clearing. 'Why would they stop at the town field,' Gelda wondered as she pulled up under a small grove with a thick and low canopy that hid her car well. Before anyone could speculate, the park filled with bright light and the hound emerged from the dark to bounce around, spin in circles, and leap up to catch unsuspecting glowflies.

'A beast in size, not nature,' Bryll remarked.

From the darkness emerged two of the uniformed Gorgons that their superiors had called trievers. The first one put dirt in the ball and set the coordinates, then they played with the hound for a few minutes. The first triever threw a stick and the second one pretended to chase it, giving the hound an extra incentive.

'Come here, Mutt!' one called. 'Over here, Mutt!' called the other, causing the hound to dart from one to the other.

'They named it?' wondered Hazzy.

'It seems so. Are they're *playing* with it?'

It was baffling to the Leffels who wondered why the Gorgons weren't attempting to get away with the stolen Cosmo Dome.

'What a lark!' said Bryll.

'Is it me or is that thing getting bigger?' Bryll said as Mutt began to morph.

'And shinier,' said Gelda.

In the dark, Mutt's coat developed a deep sheen as it turned from being hair to bioportal matter.

'What's happening to its mouth?' Hazzy wondered.

Where Mutt's mouth had been a moment ago was now a gaping hole that appeared to swallow him. It grew larger until there was nothing left that resembled a dog.

'A portal!' Hazzy had travelled a few portals, though never one that came out of a hound. 'That's how they got here.'

'A dog portal?' wondered Gelda.

'A bioportal.' Tolbert was a little impressed but mostly worried.

'I've never heard of such a thing.'

They watched the black-clad female stand guard at the side of the bioportal. When the other two reached her, the hairy one took out the capsule.

Gelda threw open the door and ran into the field. 'Give me back my Cosmo Dome!'

Bryll, Hazzy, and Tolbert hurried after her.

As Gelda closed in on them, in a sudden turn of events, the mean-faced Captain snatched the capsule from the commander's hand then jumped through the bioportal.

'Devious farker!' The commander hollered and jumped through after him.

'FIERCE! FORCE!' yelled the deputy commander.

The door of the long black vehicle slammed, and the remaining two trievers sauntered across the field. 'Run!' They ran right past Gelda and her friends to be ushered roughly through the bioportal by the deputy commander who jumped through after them.

The thump of a car door extinguished the bright light, leaving only the muted and mysterious glow of the bioportal. Screeching tires broke the silence as the black car sped away.

Gelda approached the bioportal and peered inside. The tongue walkway glistened with slobber. The fleshy mouth lining was streaked with gaps that stretched to a vortex. The stench forced her head back. It crossed her mind to jump through, but she hesitated. The bioportal hovered momentarily as a vortex, turned dog-shaped, then faded.

'Who are they?' said Bryll.

Confused, Gelda looked to him, then to where he pointed. Beyond the fading bioportal stood four strangers.

SEVENTEEN
One Down, One To Go

Being spat out of a hound had been slobberier than Ludor expected it to be. At its best, slobber was slimy, but churned up inside a bioportal, it became frothy and tacky and hard to wipe off.

'Keep your eyes and mouth shut and put your hands over your ears, otherwise you'll be digging slobber out of cavities for weeks,' Captain had warned before leaving for Equion in the Leffon territories. 'If the hound has licked its butt or eaten something nasty in the last twenty-four hours, there's not much you can do other than take a long shower with some heavy-duty cleaner afterwards. If you feel the need to puke while you're in there, don't.'

'This is so not what I signed up for,' Debrov had complained.

'What did you sign up for?' Ludor had challenged, but she didn't say.

Neither Ludor nor Debrov expected the cold wet texture or the pulling sensation. It was like getting sucked through a tight slippery tunnel. Lucky for them, on arrival in Equion it was raining, so they stood in the field and let the clean and fresh downpour wash away the slobber. Rain in Equion was nothing like the sludgy downpour in Trongarl. The hound had definitely eaten something dodgy in recent times, as a rotten stench lingered until their clothes dried.

While disturbing, their departing jaunt from Dirt City turned out to be much less of a traumatic experience than their return. The very moment before they arrived, Mutt took a rather large and steamy dump. As they hadn't yet been spat out, it was an intimate and unforgettable experience that made them all puke several times, and then some more.

'Does every time,' SHARP grumbled.

'And no one thought to warn us?' Debrov glared at SHARP.

Ludor doubted anyone could prepare for the vile experience.

'Where's Captain?' Debrov asked.

SHARP pointed up.

'Farker went to the tower without us!' Debrov fumed.

Ludor cupped his head in his hands. Now he'd have to find another way to hustle his release pass. The job had been a complete waste of time.

After everyone stopped puking, they headed inside. They cleaned up and went to the common room to await further instructions while Ludor returned Mutt to the cell. The hound wandered around sniffing the floor, then Ludor patted his thigh and the hound bounded over, tail wagging. When he rubbed his head the sensation of his hand against soft hair felt so comforting, he didn't know what to think or feel. Ludor scratched behind his ears then pushed him playfully away. The wagging spread from the tail to the whole body and the hound woofed. Ludor laughed.

'What the hell?'

He turned to see Debrov's narrowed eyes glaring at him.

'What?' he snapped as if his behaviour was totally acceptable.

'If I were you, I'd be more interested in saving my head than playing with a hound, but that's just me.' She thrust her aid in his face, and he read a message forwarded from Captain to Naye: *I've retrieved the toy. It's safe in my possession.* 'Farker's taking the cred.'

With a sigh, Ludor locked Mutt in the cell and led them to the lift. Up they went. In the executive reception, Captain was just about to swipe his tag to enter Boss King's office.

'Hey, Farktard! What's the deal?' Debrov stormed over to Captain and stood in full dominating stance, rising to full height and sticking out her chest and arms with fists locked. 'You snatched it from Commander.'

Captain smirked. 'After he did fark all.'

'His senses found the thing!' Debrov barely managed to keep a level voice.

'Then lost it.' Captain extended his smirk to Ludor. 'Losing your touch, Commander?' He swiped his tag. The door opened and in he went.

Debrov started to take a step forward, but Ludor got to her before she followed Captain inside. He put a hand on her arm. She pushed it aside, held her place, and glowered at Ludor. 'What the fark? I was about to pummel that arsehole!'

'Let's just see how this pans out,' Ludor appeased in a tone just short of being condescending. Though grateful she was siding with him, he understood that she expected him to side back, but he cared little about grudges and griping and knew she'd feel differently if she knew his real reason for being on the job.

Naye waved them over and shared what had been happening at HQ since they'd been gone. 'His Royal Sir has had the full treatment and now looks like a badass. They showed them a picture of Boss King. There was no trace of the man who had let himself go that Ludor had seen the previous day. He looked good – almost too good. 'There's a barrel of top shelf brew on the way, and the party crew are almost done setting up the gala. Apparently, they've found some gnarly party weapons. It's going to be volatile as hell.'

'Least the job will end well,' said Debrov.

Ludor had to agree. Getting messed up on some top shelf brew was a fine way of appeasing his frustrations.

Naye indicated a speaker under the reception bench and nodded towards Boss King's office with a cheeky grin. Together, they listened in.

Predictably, Captain told Boss King that he was the one to find and retrieve the toy, going as far as to say, 'Royal Sir, I took it upon myself to personally carry it here to ensure its safe delivery. No one else has touched it and nothing damaged it on the journey. You'll be pleased to know it's in immaculate condition.'

'Good. Hand it over.' There was a long moment of silence. Then Boss King said in a slow and low voice, 'Is this some kind of joke?'

There was a pause, then Captain stammered, 'Is there a

problem?'

'A problem?!' Boss King's tone escalated to shrill level. 'This is some old broken shitty model. It's not even a Universe, probably a Jinverse, for farksake. What the hell are you playing at, you dumb fark?!'

Naye stifled a laugh and whispered, 'Oh, this is bad, even for Captain. Royal Sir hasn't done a beheading in ages. What a riot!'

Debrov chuckled quietly. 'He'll end up head-jarred for sure.' Grinning wildly, she plonked herself down on the couch with her feet on the lounge table. Perhaps her smugness needed cushioning, but she never sat on a job. She jabbed at her aide and navigated to the public feed.

The noises coming from Boss King's office were wild and varied. Naye switched off the intercom halfway through when they all agreed they knew where it was heading.

While Ludor was pleased that Captain was getting what he deserved, the missing toy played on his mind. Had they been duped by the Leffels? 'I guess we're interviewing for a new captain and heading back to Leffon.' He sighed. 'We're back where we started.'

'Not quite. Seems we have another interested party.' Debrov showed Ludor footage from the Equion restaurant on her aide. A petite person in an oversized coat and wearing a cap down low over their eyes, drifted towards the table while they studied the menus. In a move so smooth it took a few watches to notice, the coat opened, and another capsule replaced the Universe in Captain's lap. The thief walked on unseen.

'So we had the real one.' Ludor studied the footage again. 'And another Leffel took it.'

Debrov pointed at hair showing through the bottom of the cap. 'And we know who.'

Ludor nodded. The girl with the green streak of hair at the house. Shellany. 'Good work, Deputy. Do a trace.'

'On it.'

The intercom buzzed and Boss King said, 'Send in the medics with a stretcher and a head box.'

'Called it,' Naye whispered to them.

'And tell Commander to come in.'

Ah, fark, thought Ludor. This could go either way.

'You're good.' Naye wasn't worried. 'His Royal Sir knows the look of someone who's farked up bad, and Captain's had it coming for a while.' They unlocked the door and in Ludor went.

Ludor couldn't decide if the office was worse or better. A bad smell still lingered, but it wasn't anything like the cloying stench it was before. The sagging couch had been replaced with a rather posh looking chaise and the large box-shaped stain on the oak wall was covered by a new painting. It was tidy but the blood and brains splattered on the walls and over the recently cleaned carpet really added an unpleasant touch to the shine and sparkle.

He stepped over the beheaded body dripping blood and oozing innards. Reaching for the chair, he almost kicked the dislodged head that had half rolled under the desk but was soon uncomfortably seated.

The fancy glass cabinet with brass frames still took up most of the space on the desk but without the papers, stationery, and dirty kitchenware. Pushed to one end, it was turned sideways so Ludor could see Boss King clearly. He was dressed in a black suit embedded with tiny diamonds that glittered and sparkled. His clean and glossy hair was cut short to complement his new chiselled and clean-shaved jawline. Muscle replaced the flab that previously drooped over the chair arms. There was a radiant shine to his skin and eyes. Taut and healthy suited him.

'What the fark happened out there?' Boss King demanded to know.

To keep things simple, Ludor told him an account laced with lies then quickly divulged a new plan to take his attention from failures to potential successes. Boss King listened with a frown while staring at the cabinet.

'Didn't you even look at the farking thing before you took it?'

'I'm not an idiot! It was the same as the image.'

'So it somehow morphed into a shitty one?'

'I don't know what happened, 'Ludor lied, 'But I'll find out.'

Boss King seethed. 'You'd better. This is your last chance, Commander. Get my Universe or else that'll be you.' Boss King nodded his head to Captain's that lay severed on the carpet.

Ludor thought about mentioning his release pass again, but Boss King loathed it when someone stopped him from revelling in his own importance, and beheadings often came in twos. Getting out of the firing line was the smart option. The time for negotiating was when he had the toy.

The stretchers arrived then left with Captain's body on one, his head on the other. Ludor waited for permission to leave then did. Back in reception Naye had gone home, and Debrov stood there looking intimidating but really just in guard mode.

'What happens to your brain when you're standing there like that?'

Debrov shrugged. 'It just goes into auto-vigilant mode. I'm relaxed but alert at the same time.' She filled him in on the latest. 'Captain's body's gone to medical and his head's gone to the DNA incinerator.'

Ludor knew the drill. It took too long for a new head to grow back so Captain would be assigned another one from the company headmaker.

'There's not much chance of his new head being uglier than the old one, but he's going to make a damn fine shitkicker,' Debrov speculated.

'No one's going to be looking at him where he's going,' replied Ludor. Clearing out blockages from the sewerage canals was where most of Boss King's disgraced A-team ended up, or someplace even more banal.

They left HQ together.

'Get some shut eye,' he told his deputy at the gates. 'Tomorrow, we head back to Leffon.'

Before heading down the ditchwalk that would take him home, he turned to see Giorana exit the building and move in the opposite direction. *When this is all over, I'm going to follow her until I see her face,* he swore, *but not at dawn. Sleep calls.*

EIGHTEEN
Tricky Intel

Gelda fiddled with her aide to get some light. Before she found it, the area behind where the bioportal had been lit up brightly. She looked up to see one of the four strangers pointing his aide light at the ground between them. He was tall and thin, wearing a yellow cap and bow tie, and stood a step ahead of the others.

'Tawawa!' He delivered the greeting with sincerity and respect. 'I'm curious about how you came to possess my Universe.' He seemed simultaneously tired and wired.

Gelda stepped forward. 'Tawawa! *Your* Universe?'

'It was stolen.'

'How awful!' Gelda gasped and expressed her consternation with a shake of her head. 'And now it's been stolen again!'

'Tawawa!' greeted a shorter man with thick lips and pudgy hands. 'We think it's the one you had that the Gorgons just took. It's all very confusing.'

'It is,' Gelda agreed. 'And odd.'

'Tawawa!' A lithe, pale short-haired woman stepped into the light next to the tall man. 'Did you buy it from them and they stole it back?'

'I absolutely did not buy it from them!' Gelda assured them. 'I bought it from the Marvellus Amusements Exchange.'

'Tawawa!' Bryll greeted. 'Were you in that town van?'

'Tawawa!' Hazzy said. 'Or the hovermobile?'

'Tawawa! There was a hovermobile?' The petite woman projected dormant energy, as though she was ready for adventure at any given moment. 'Oh, I'd love to ride in one!'

'Me, too!' Gelda said, and the others murmured in agreement. 'It would be most helpful to know who you are. We are locals. Are you?'

'We are,' said the tall man with the cap and bowtie. His darting eyes could be mistaken for nervousness or an expectation that something unexpected was about to happen, but the lips that curled up on the ends indicated a person who liked to be prepared.

'Tawawa! We're wasting time.' The short man tapped the pudgy fingers of both hands together while he spoke, giving the impression of a deep thinker shuffling ideas around in his head as his brain raced towards solutions. 'We should be on our way to Gorgonia by now.'

'Tawawa! We don't know their destination.' The fourth stranger, a man in a long pink-and-green coat and purple boots emerged from willowy smoke. It dispersed as quickly as it appeared from a long and narrow pipe held with two fingers to the side of his face. 'And how? We don't have a portal.'

That caused another round of debating.

'Evidently we all want to get the Universe back, so how about we work together?' said the smoker in the coat and boots.

'You mean form an allegiance?' Hazzy asked.

'We should at least discuss the matter,' said the thinker.

They all agreed a collaboration was just what they needed.

Lanseth introduced himself with a tip of his yellow cap, then introduced his group. Prinn was the petite and upbeat woman, Renoy was the one in the coloured coat smoking the pipe, and Alrick was the fidgeting thinker.

After the Leffels introduced themselves, Gelda realised Tolbert was missing. She turned and spotted him standing between them and the vehicle with his head down. As the two groups got acquainted, Gelda left to find out why he hadn't joined them and found him caught up tinkering with his tracking device and talking to himself or someone she couldn't see again. He didn't even notice her until she spoke. 'Is something wrong?'

Frowning, he shook his head. 'I'm not sure. I'm just checking the operating system. The thing is, I set it to maximum distance which should cover Gorgonia, but it's not moving from here. I can't find a fault.'

'Maybe the Gorgons hacked your system?'

'I doubt they'd have the smarts for that.' He glanced over at the strangers. 'The Domers could help.'

'Who?'

'The group you're talking with are massive Cosmo Dome fans

who would do anything to protect them. I don't know them personally, but I know all about them.'

Gelda noticed that he looked at the same spot again. She saw nothing and wondered what he saw or didn't see.

He put the cover back on the tracker and held it up. 'It seems I can't get this working, so we need a Plan B.'

'Then let's talk with them.'

When they got there, Renoy stared intently at Tolbert. He puffed at his pipe, blew out blue smoke. The pungent herbs dispersed so that everyone breathed in their pungent aroma. 'You're familiar. What's your name?'

'I invented Cosmo Dome,' Tolbert admitted. Before the oohh's and aahh's that followed turned into words that would distract all from the task, he added, 'We clearly have a lot to discuss but not here.'

'Somewhere safe,' agreed the one called Prinn.

'What about that restaurant?' suggested Gelda who still craved something more than a light snack to appease her growing hunger.

Lanseth's aide pinged. He consulted it then looked up whitefaced. 'We need to go to the club,' he said then added, 'all of us.'

Renoy put the pipe in a metal case and dropped it into his coat pocket. 'She's back?'

'On her way over.'

'She's got some explaining to do.'

'Who's on her way over to explain what?' Hazzy enquired.

'We have intel at our clubhouse. It's not too far from here,' was all Lanseth would say.

Tolbert looked up from the tracking device. 'Does this intel have something to do with the Universe?'

'I would imagine so,' said Lanseth.

Prinn gave Gelda the clubhouse address, then the two parties split up back to their vehicles.

'What the heck is going on?' Bryll wondered as they piled back in the car.

'I don't know, but I guess we're about to find out,' said Gelda.

'Have you got your tracker working again?' Gelda asked Tolbert as they got in the car.

He shook his head. 'It's still giving a local reading.'

'Then let's hope this leads somewhere.'

She drove at top speed away from the field.

NINETEEN

A Confession and a Plan

By the time Gelda and friends arrived in Alkupera Town, noon was almost upon them. People busied themselves going in and out of buildings and vehicles, most stopping several times to chat, all bearing smiles and warm greetings. The temperature was mild, the air fragrancers had come and gone, and the prettiest tiny red and yellow fleurs were in bloom. It was another lovely day.

For the entire trip, Tolbert had been consumed with the tracking device and commenting on how it seemed like it was following them rather than the other way around. 'This confounding thing is really on the blink,' he said as they rounded the corner onto the street of the address. 'Now it's defaulted back to its home location.'

Gelda couldn't help but occasionally glance back at him as she drove to see he still chatted to the space ahead of him. He was indeed an odd man.

The Domers League clubhouse was on a busy street near the town centre. A block away from the address Prinn gave them, the car made strange gurgling noises, offered up a few clunks, then the engine packed it in.

'And there it goes,' Gelda mournfully sang.

'Oh, dear!' Hazzy commiserated. 'It almost made it. That's something.'

'That's something indeed,' replied Gelda.

Gelda steered the vehicle to the side of the road as it rolled to a stop. They got out and looked for signs of the cause but saw nothing.

'No point in wasting time on it.' Gelda led them the remaining distance to the club. It was a two-storey building with a pink and green 'Patik's Best Couries In Town' sign emblazoned above an ornate door at the front. Next to it was a small red arrow with 'Domers Club' handwritten in yellow that indicated to go round the side. They walked down a narrow alley and up a flight of metal stairs around the back to a locked dark-green wooden door. Gelda pressed a small round button where a door handle might've been.

'Hello?' came Lanseth's voice from the speaker.

'Tawawa! It's Gelda and friends.'

'Tawawa, Gelda, and friends!' The door clicked open. They entered a small empty foyer, then an internal door opened ahead.

Lanseth greeted them with a smile and was about to say something when a voice from behind said, 'Who wants breakfast?'

They turned to see Alrick holding a basket of pastries and fruit. The sweet aroma made mouths water and stomachs grumble. They followed him inside a large room that had six gaming cubicles backed up against each other in two rows of three in front of a partition wall covered in maps, notes, diagrams, and schedules. Alrick placed the basket on a bench in a kitchen area where Renoy was making jova.

Prinn appeared from a door next to the window. 'Tawawa!' they greeted each other.

Hazzy went to the window to look out while Tolbert disappeared around the partition wall.

'Hungry?' Lanseth asked Gelda and Bryll.

Gelda's stomach grumbled. She thought it polite to only take a light puffly until Alrick said, 'Try a sugar ring. Oh, and definitely a liosh bredde. They're from my mother's bakery.'

'They're the flakiest pastries in town,' Renoy said with his mouth full.

'And she grows the best berries,' Lanseth told them, arranging large and luscious redberries, freshly picked zingberries, and brightly coloured speckleberries into a bowl, then selecting a liosh bredde from the basket.

Gelda poured jova into a bright orange cup then selected the recommended sugar ring and flake wrap, while Bryll chose a sweetspice scroll and a puffly twist coated in shoka and nibbleberries. The pastries were melt-in-the-mouth delicious and the jova was full-bodied and smooth. Jovas in hand, they followed Lanseth past the gaming stations to a rest area behind the partition wall. Lounge chairs surrounded a round lowset table.

Tolbert already sat in one, tinkering with the tracking device and chatting to SID. When he saw them, he said, 'It's not the most robust device I've invented, but I do have a sort of portal—'

'A portal? Why didn't you say?' Alrick had only just sat down, but now he jumped up. 'Let's go!'

Tolbert waved his enthusiasm aside. 'It's more of a space gate, and it's of no use without coordinates and what about the intel we're here for?'

Lanseth checked his aide. 'She should be here by now.' Just as he said it, in walked Shellany.

'Shellany?' said Gelda and Tolbert at the same time.

Everyone exchanged looks of confusion.

'You know each other?' Lanseth asked Tolbert and Shellany the same question Gelda and her friends also wanted answered.

Shellany's eyes moved from Lanseth to Tolbert to Gelda. Instead of answering, she unzipped a pack and presented a capsule with a zig-zag pattern.

Gelda gasped. 'My Universe?' Lanseth shot a glance at her so she added, 'I mean the missing Universe?'

With a curt nod, Shellany placed it gently on the table.

'What?' Lanseth exhaled the word.

Renoy donned a doubtful frown. 'How?'

Shellany's hand went up to silence any further questions. She took a deep breath. 'When I first came to the club, I told you I was a Cosmo Dome fan, and I am – kind of – but that's not the reason I joined.' She looked at Tolbert when she said that. 'It wasn't to play. It was to steal the Universe.'

'What?' Lanseth coughed and almost choked on his puffly.

'B-But we're friends!' Prinn stammered.

'You betrayed us?!' said Alrick.

Gelda and friends watched the conversation play out to piece it together.

'I don't understand,' said Lanseth. 'We welcome you into our club and even offer you a Jinverse to play, and you steal a Universe?'

'Not just any Universe – the *last* one.' Renoy looked almost as fierce as a Gorgon.

'I'm sure she had her reasons,' Gelda soothed. 'Let's not forget she brought it back.' She gave Shellany a smile of encouragement, and they learnt that she'd been hired by the Gorgon former Boss Queen, Giorana, to find it.

'I regretted it immediately and even pleaded with her to let me have it back when it was clear she had no use for it. I didn't know she'd listed it on the Marvellus exchange until you did.' She addressed Lanseth when she said that. 'When you tracked it down, I followed you to Gelda's then took it from the Gorgons at the restaurant. I went in disguise and made sure I wasn't followed.'

'You still haven't said why,' said Lanseth quietly.

'I was angry over something that has nothing to do with you.' Shellany glanced Tolbert's way. Tears welled as she forced herself to make eye contact with everyone in the room. 'It's the worst thing I've ever done. I am fond of you all and I am so sorry.' Their hurt and anger was punishing. 'I don't expect your forgiveness, but my hope is bringing it back will at least ease your distress.' She turned and left.

'That's it?' Lanseth stood and called out as Shellany reached the edge of the partition wall. When Shellany turned, he added, 'You steal a Universe, bring it back, say sorry, and then leave?'

'What else is there?'

'Forgiveness?' Prinn joined Lanseth at the wall edge. 'We're still your friends.'

'There's no need to leave,' Alrick encouraged from his seat.

Bryll shrugged. 'You helped Gelda fix and play Cosmo Dome, so you're obviously a good person.'

'And did a stellar job of it, too.' Gelda beamed.

'Nothing's ever so bad it can't be fixed by a cup of kerai.' Hazzy skittered off into the kitchen to brew some.

Renoy's expression went from angry to blank. Then he gave a curt nod. 'I get it. I've done shitty things too.'

Lanseth looked up from staring into his empty cup and gave a soft smile. 'It takes courage to own your mistakes.'

Tolbert was the only one not to offer encouragement. He kept his head down and rubbed thumbs over curled up fists.

Shellany stood motionless in a fight-or-flight conundrum. Leaving was the easy option. Staying was the right thing to do, but the awkwardness was unbearable.

'Don't go,' Lanseth said quietly. 'The Jinverse still needs a player, and we'd miss you.'

With all eyes on her, Shellany forced her legs to return her to everyone. She sat down in a vacant chair. The capsule lay untouched on the table. No one spoke. The looks between

Shellany and Tolbert didn't go unnoticed.

'Tell them the whole truth,' Tolbert encouraged softly.

Shellany stared at him for a long moment. 'My surname is Shimble.' No one understood the significance.

'She's my daughter,' Tolbert told them, then said to Shellany in a matter-of-fact tone, 'You stole the Universe to get back at me.'

'I knew you'd hate a Gorgon overlord being the first to complete a set, especially one with its biospheres severed,' Shellany confessed.

'I left to protect you,' he said, though the words felt profoundly insufficient.

'You broke our family.'

'I'm sorry,' Tolbert said almost inaudibly.

Lanseth got up and motioned for the others to do the same. They congregated in the foyer to give the estranged pair a moment alone. No one spoke but many yawned. After what seemed to be an eternity, Tolbert appeared at the door. 'Thanks. I feel responsible for her actions and appreciate your kindness.'

Lanseth smiled. 'Of course.'

Everyone dragged their weary bodies back into the rest area and they got to discussing what to do next.

'They'll be back,' said Shellany.

'How did you happen to have the last Universe anyway?' Tolbert put to Lanseth.

'Good question,' Gelda agreed.

'And why wasn't it played?' Tolbert asked.

'It was mine,' Lanseth confessed. 'I ordered it when I lost my first Essaverse but couldn't get past the glitch.'

'The glitch?' Gelda queried. She kept hearing the term and was eager to know more.

'So you reset it?' Tolbert asked at the same time.

'I did,' Lanseth confessed. Head down, he turned away.

'Resetting a game restores it to pre-initiation,' Shellany explained to Gelda and her friends.

'Which means a biosphere reverts to its original state. It's rarely done.' Tolbert added.

Lanseth looked up with remorse clear in his sad eyes and tight lips. 'It seems appalling, I know, but I had hoped to overcome the glitch.'

What is the glitch everyone keeps talking about?! Gelda had to know. She also desperately wanted to discuss what had happened to her inside the Universe on PEACH, but the conversation took its own direction.

'It would have perished otherwise,' said Alrick.

'None of us were up to the challenge of playing it after that so we made a group decision to lock it away until a worthy player came along,' said Renoy.

'And no one did,' Prinn added quietly.

'Until you,' Shellany said to Gelda. 'I didn't mean to deceive you. I honestly came to warn you about the Gorgons and explain that it shouldn't have been on the market in the first place, but when I knocked on the door someone pulled me inside and handed me a decanter of very good elixir. Everyone was crowded around the Universe having such fun. I guess I got caught in the excitement and saw the opportunity to save it by you playing the construction levels so Boss King couldn't sever it. It seemed the perfect solution, but it was misleading. I should have just told you the truth.'

Gelda shook her head. 'If you had told me all of that I probably would have shoved it in your face and asked you to leave.'

'You would not!' said Hazzy. 'You're much too polite for that.'

'Perhaps, but I wouldn't have played it, but I did, and now here we are and I'm glad. To be honest, I'm more concerned about this glitch you all keep talking about. What is it?!' *Not to mention finding myself inside the Universe,* she wanted to add, but one thing at a time.

Tolbert shook his hand and sighed. 'It's an anomaly that seems to have infected all the Universes. There's no pattern to it at all.'

'First thing's first,' said Shellany. 'As much as I'd like to think our trouble with the Gorgons is over, they won't give up, which means they'll be back to retrieve the Universe very soon.'

'Exactly, and the only way to stop them from wanting it is to finish construction,' said Tolbert. He looked to Gelda. 'Do you think you have what it takes to play?'

'She definitely does,' said Shellany.

'I hope so,' Gelda replied.

'Trust me. You have what it takes,' Shellany affirmed.

'Good, good,' said Tolbert. 'And the glitch?'

With eyes closed, Shellany nodded. 'It's appeared.'

'It has?' said Gelda.

'Let me guess: a planet in a distant galaxy?' said Tolbert.

'Yep,' replied Shellany.

'It's always a planet,' Tolbert lamented. 'Will you code?'

While Shellany suspected her father suggested it to win her favour, she also wanted to make amends to the club and to help. If she could prove herself a worthy Domer, perhaps they would still have her. 'Of course,' she said simply. It had been a long few days and she was done with talking.

'So, it's decided,' said Lanseth. 'You'll fix the glitch and Gelda will finish construction so that the Gorgons can't stop it.'

'Just like that,' muttered Shellany.

'Are you okay with that?' Gelda asked Lanseth. 'I mean it was your game before it was mine.'

'I'm just glad it's in the right hands.' Lanseth smiled encouragingly.

'Let's get started.' Shellany headed for the game stations, but Lanseth called her back.

'Not here,' he said. 'It's not safe. The Gorgons only have to search the public feed and they'll find the club. It's the most obvious place to begin their search.'

'Then where?' Gelda wondered.

'My place on Anon,' said Tolbert.

'Isn't that a secluded world?' said Hazzy.

'Exactly. It's the last place anyone would look.'

'It's too far away,' said Gelda. 'We don't have time or energy for a long trip right now.'

'Fortunately, you require neither.' Tolbert reached into his satchel and took out the space compactor. He fastened the disc to his waist again, then pressed the buttons to make the pulsating transparent rings.

'A portal?' Hazzy admired the swirling colours rippling across its surface.

'Broadly yes, but it uses a unique space-time method that compresses the layers of reality from departure to destination. The jaunt is a tad disorientating, but it got me here. I call it the space compactor.' It looked like Tolbert just stopped talking to look into the space ahead as SID's waveform fluctuated.

'You should call it the spactor,' SID said. Being mobile meant limited processes so she was only seen and heard by Tolbert.

'An abridgement. Great idea,' he agreed and smiled innocently at the people around him. 'I'm calling it the spactor.'

'It's small,' Renoy remarked.

'It's a prototype. Travel capacity is limited to one person at a time – two if you don't require an immediate return. Initial charge takes a while, then it needs to recharge between jumps.'

'It will take ages for us all to get through,' said Prinn woefully.

'You go. We'll stay here,' Alrick suggested.

Renoy objected. 'It won't be long before the Gorgons crash down the door.'

'We can't leave our Cosmo Domes,' said Prinn.

'Or anything that proves we were here or where we've gone,' said Alrick.

Lanseth sighed and paced about. 'We pack them up, clear the place out, then go.'

'Will you come back for us?' Alrick asked Shellany.

'Of course,' she said, happy that she was forgiven and of use.

'Then it's sorted,' said Lanseth. 'You three go and we'll message you when we're ready to join you.'

Hazzy and Bryll were chatting near the window, but they came back and Hazzy said, 'Odgio's coming with Fansy and Finkle.'

'I'm so glad you're all coming with us!' said Gelda. Tolbert's spactor contraption would be put to good use transporting them all to Anon. She just hoped they would all get off-world before the Gorgons found them.

Hazzy shook her head. 'No, love. They're coming to collect us.' She squeezed Gelda's hand. 'It's best if we stay in Equion.'

'What? No! You must come to Anon. What an adventure it will be!'

'*Your* adventure, my dear friend. Go and enjoy.'

'She's right, Ma Varda,' Bryll agreed. 'We'd be surplus. Go save your game.'

Hazzy hugged Gelda tightly. 'Let us know if you need anything. Worst case, I can get hold of a portal or book a flyover.'

'Are you sure?'

'Absolutely! You have a grand project to accomplish and good support. It's a wonderful gift. Enjoy it!'

Gelda walked them both out and they said their goodbyes, just as Odgio and Fansy arrived with Finkle.

Finkle wriggled in his travel pouch to get out. Gelda unzipped the top for head kisses. 'Be good for Hazzy,' she told him.

'Bit of an escapade you're embarking upon,' said Odgio with a wink and wished her luck.

Fansy leaned in and whispered in Gelda's ear, 'Remember, it's just a game. Though I am curious to see how it all turns out.' She laughed.

'You're trouble, Aunt Fansy,' Gelda teased.

'Keep your aide on and update us!' Bryll called out.

Hands waved and kisses blown, they departed. Gelda reeled in their residual energy, then went back inside. Ignoring the faintly pulsating compression rings of the spactor's initial charge, the Domers sat around the table talking in faint whispers. Gelda sat next to Lanseth who turned and smiled. 'It's not the best of circumstances, but I'm so glad we've met. The club has been searching for a Universe player for ages, but there has been no one good enough to pass the glitch.'

'Don't get too excited. A faulty planet keeps stopping me

from passing levels,' Gelda admitted.

'It's a thing,' said Prinn, as though she was an expert on the matter.

'It's true,' Lanseth agreed. 'All players of Universe experience it.'

'That's the glitch?' Gelda wondered.

'Probably,' said Tolbert. 'I analysed it for decades and never figured it out.' He smiled at the Domers. 'I have to say, it's really great to finally meet you all.'

'Same!' Prinn said.

'It's an honour to meet you.' Lanseth looked a tad starstruck.

'Very much so,' Alrick agreed. 'We didn't know who you were at first, so we were quite suspicious when we saw you at Gelda's house.'

'You were in the bright town van?' asked Gelda.

'We were on a stake-out,' Prinn said.

'We thought you might be Gorgons,' Renoy confessed.

When Gelda laughed at the thought, so did they.

'And then when you turned up, we wondered if you were a collector,' Renoy said to Tolbert.

'Never in a trillion years did we think you'd be the inventor,' said Lanseth.

Tolbert laughed. 'How did you even track the Universe?'

'Alrick hacked your System,' Lanseth told him. 'He's our tech genius.'

'Only your notifications.' Alrick said quickly. He didn't want Tolbert thinking he was meddlesome or disrespectful.

'I'm impressed you got that far.' Tolbert made a mental note to ask SID about the incident. The mobile system was running low on power and so he kept their communication to necessary only.

'Lanseth has the most cultivated Essaverse in Leffon,' Prinn boasted. 'That's why he's club president.'

'Don't forget head judge at CosmoCon,' Alrick said.

'I formed the club from winners of each model,' admitted Lanseth.

'That's us,' said Prinn proudly. 'Want to see our biospheres?'

Dog-tired, the two guests were nevertheless eager. Prinn led them over to the long windows behind the lounge and unlocked the six white locker cabinets to unveil the biospheres.

Renoy was first to take his out. The Bonverse was a testament to simplicity. The biosphere was white with occasional dark spots. He hooked up the controller and projected it in the display. On a white background floated transparent creatures that were mostly bulbous with multiple spikes or nodules. They ranged from large to so small that Renoy had to zoom in for them to see. 'The more you zoom, the more you see,' he explained and zoomed in on a bulging lifeform that contained lifeforms, and they too contained lifeforms, and so on.

'Breathtaking,' said Gelda. 'What do they do?'

'Explore, connect, and multiply,' said Renoy. 'It's a subtle game that suits my groove.'

'It's definitely your pace,' Gelda said. 'What status have you reached?'

'Custodian.'

'We've all finished the construction levels,' said Lanseth.

'Now we watch and care,' said Prinn.

'It's a big responsibility,' said Renoy.

'But rewarding,' said Alrick.

'It's frustrating when something goes wrong and you can't fix it,' said Renoy.

Prinn went next with Thalverse. Mostly blue and green, it had swirling patterns of cloudy areas interspersed with bold stripes or dots. She projected the display for a closer look at abundant and varied aquatic life that was calming and enticing.

'I could look at it for days,' Gelda whispered.

'It's relaxing, isn't it?' Prinn agreed. 'I have two, but my other one is in the healing incubator recovering from an infection.'

'Tawawa! I hope it's okay.'

Alrick took his out. 'Wellaverse was the first biosphere to have separate worlds. Check out the colours and textures.' It was mostly black with some green and blue and patches of warmer tones. Its display revealed a few hundred worlds. Zooming in on a planet revealed the warm tones as rocky terrain and vast plains. Two- and four-legged lifeforms moved or settled in small groups or wandered alone.

'I prefer my worlds to have pristine environments, and since there aren't many civilisations, I focus on innovation as a means of evolution, rather than reproduction. It means each world has a better chance of survival without risk of overpopulation.'

'Alrick is a diligent problem solver,' Lanseth said.

'He's played Wellaverse to perfection,' Renoy praised his club mate.

Lanseth's Essaverse was mostly black with some blue and white. Revealed in the display, the intricacies of galaxies became apparent. Spaced far apart, they were simple clusters of sprawling dust, gas, dark matter, and a few thousand stars, all held together by gravity. Zooming in on a planet revealed a solid, active surface with mountains, valleys, canyons, plains, and so much more. Lanseth pulled up a screen with categories: habitability, location, sustainability, and species survival.

Both Gelda and Tolbert enjoyed seeing the differences and how each player put their own stamp on their biospheres.

'What about the Jinverse?' Tolbert gave the remaining model a head nod.

Lanseth said, 'It was donated to us by a player who had other commitments off-world. Prinn has been its caretaker for quite some time now.'

'It's lovely and I don't mind at all, but it deserves someone to care for it properly,' Prinn interjected.

'Shellany was going to play it,' said Lanseth.

'Before I messed up,' Shellany said quietly.

Before anyone could comment, the spactor said, 'This way is open' and repeated the message between two long pauses filled with bleeps. The large button in its centre flashed a lit-up green *Open*.

'It's charged. Ready to go?' Tolbert asked Gelda and Shellany.

'I don't have anything with me.' Gelda hadn't expected to be gone for days and had no change of clothes. She was still in her party gown, and her feet were sore from the fancy shoes.

'No problem. We can get you whatever you need.' Tolbert adjusted the spactor settings on his aide. 'It will need to power up after each jump, but only for a fraction of the time of the first charge. When I say go, step through fast.'

'Let me know when you're ready, and I'll come back to collect you,' Shellany told the Domers.

They said their farewells. The spactor bleeped and recited its message once last time then, one by one, off they went.

TWENTY
Sharp as a Sponge

Rain turned dust to sludge the morning Ludor returned to HQ. In the ditchwalk, his squelching boots splashed mud up a heavy grey coat already turned dark from the torrent. Hands shoved in pockets, he marched fast, wanting the day over and hoping against odds for an efficient retrieval of the Leffel toy.

'Outta way, farker!'

He narrowly dodged getting hit by a cart, no doubt steered by drunken and sleepy brawlers who had most likely programmed it incorrectly. A brief thought about yelling abuse back crossed his mind, but he really couldn't be bothered.

There were several more brawls than the previous day to take care of. Not sure whether to be reassured or disappointed by a return to the usual goings-on, he wasn't in the mood for a distraction. It only took a few minutes each to swiftly knock out several eager individuals who got in his way. It was easier than giving them a chance to antagonise him first. The faster the fight, the sooner he could just get on with the rest of his day and get home. It sucked being good at something you hated. Ludor sighed. The day he got off Trongarl couldn't come soon enough.

Not bothering to clean his boots or dry his coat, Ludor went straight to Basement Level 2. He'd arranged to meet Debrov and the trievers in the common room at dusk to figure shit out and get on with it before night-time. Going in or out of the hound was better when they could see, and they all wanted to get back to getting up to no good after the job.

The others hadn't arrived yet, so, Ludor headed down to Basement Level 1 to check on Mutt. Mutt's entire body waggled when he saw Ludor who felt a sudden lightness in his chest that he put down to nerves over the upcoming mission, even though nothing had made him anxious before. He scooped feed into an empty bowl, watched the hound polish it off in a couple of mouthfuls, then poured another scoop. Fed and watered, tail wagged and dripping tongue lolled. Ludor felt all warm inside. It didn't feel wrong, which meant it was, but he didn't care.

Debrov was in the common area when he got back to Basement Level 2 with Mutt on a chain. 'I hacked the restaurant surveillance and traced the perpetrator back to a vehicle with an Alkupera Town registration.' She thrust her wrist in his face, showing him a page of small type on her aide and supplemented it with a verbal info dump. 'I accessed national transport surveillance, which took me all of five seconds – it's like they never have infringements there – then traced the vehicle movements back to the house where we found it. One of those party idiots must have followed us.'

'How? BRISK drove fast.'

'Tracker?'

'Or some kind of hitech Leffel surveillance. Gather the

trievers and let's get going.' Just as Ludor said that, FORCE, BRISK, and FIERCE arrived. 'Where's SHARP?'

'Taking a hit somewhere, me thinks,' said BRISK.

'For what?' enquired Ludor.

'Thems cheated on the test,' said FIERCE.

'What test?'

'To become a triever,' said FORCE. 'Thems was assigned the Big E so nicked a more favourable result.'

'And that means what?' It was too early in the day for Ludor to decipher triever lingo.

'Means them's expandable,' said FORCE.

'Expendable, farktard,' said BRISK.

'First in, last out – if them makes it.' FIERCE ran a finger over her throat.

'Deems them fine reason to cheat soze to make assertions in a squad instead of idle for uncountable whiles.' BRISK showed them footage on his aide of SHARP-9S21 being interrogated by a lithe individual holding a leather whip in one hand and a chain with chunky links in the other. Torture ensued. There was no point to the presentation, other than entertainment value.

'Seemed SHARP was dumb as dirt.' Debrov showed Ludor more footage from the restaurant on her aide with the focus on the conspiring SHARP. Seated next to Captain, they watched the thief swap capsules and then went back to eating as though nothing had happened.

'What the fark? Did they think it was a double retrieval?'

Debrov shrugged and was about to reply when a new triever entered the room.

'SHARP-9S01 reporting for duty,' said an alert individual with white hair tied in a bun and a very neat and clean uniform.

'9S01? You was top in class for timing and aim,' BRISK recalled in admiration.

'How's you here?' asked FIERCE looking confused.

'Completed last mission in speed of schedule,' said the new SHARP, gaining tumultuous praise and many slaps on the back.

'Calm the fark down and shut the hell up.' Ludor gained back control. 'Gather your weapons and let's get going.'

'But needs new captain,' said FORCE.

Ludor nodded towards Debrov. 'Want the job?'

'Any benefits?'

'You get to order four trievers around and get free brews at their tavern afterwards.'

Debrov shrugged. 'Sold.'

Out in the courtyard, it didn't take much encouragement for Mutt to portalise and they were gone. The car provided by a top-secret Gorgon contact was already at the field. A nonbeliever in good fortune, Ludor was immediately anxious. If something seemed advantageous, it usually turned out to be quite the opposite. BRISK drove and they arrived at the house at dusk. Breaking in was as simple as opening the door, though Debrov and her trievers still smashed windows and put holes through walls.

'Finally, you're home,' grumbled the faulty message machine, assuming the activity in the kitchen was Gelda.

'Machine's got an attitude,' said Debrov, arms folded.

'It's pretty old and broke for a utilised Leffel appliance.' Ludor wondered why the place didn't have shiny new things like most Leffel homes.

'You have a new message from Fansy,' the machine continued. 'Want to hear it?'

Debrov looked questioningly towards Ludor who got what she was asking and shrugged.

'Yes,' she said.

The message played. 'Tawawa, Gelda! I can't find the Domers Club. I did, however, find a Domers League in town. Is that it? Anyway, I'm heading home to get some sleep, but I'll stay online in case you call. Love you, darling, and hope you find your game. So exciting, all this hubbub, isn't it? Stay safe. Tawawa!'

'Seems we're heading into town,' said Debrov.

They piled into the vehicle. Debrov went to sit up front, but Mutt was with him. Ludor told her to hop in the back.

'What the fark?' his former deputy and newly appointed captain complained.

'It's for security,' Ludor explained, explaining nothing.

Debrov glared at him then slammed the door. She got in the back and pushed FORCE over for space. She hated being touched, especially by trievers. Their stank lingered on her uniform and she had to wash it when she got home and it was never properly dry the next morning.

Ludor rolled the window down for Mutt to stick his big fluffy head out.

'If you start petting it, I'm reporting you,' said Debrov.

He didn't bother replying. Off they went.

TWENTY-ONE
A House in the Clouds

It wasn't anything in particular that woke Gelda. She simply opened her eyes and found herself looking out a window at large-leafed trees. Sleepily content and not at all worried, she wondered where she was and then remembered the spactor journey the night before. As her brain kicked into gear, fragmented details of the past few days cascaded through her mind in no particular order, starting with Finkle and rambling through her mind. She let it happen.

She hoped he wasn't fretting over being away from home, or wreaking havoc in Hazzy's house. The party had gone well, all things considered. By now, everyone had probably returned to their daily lives with good memories of the occasion, other than those who'd stayed behind to cheer her on. Speaking of which, she must update everyone to let them know she'd made it safely to Anon.

Raquin and Barlo would have left for their Trip of a Lifetime by now. It seemed strange that they had no idea about any of this Cosmo Dome business, but she wasn't about to worry them. The Gorgons would've probably figured out they didn't have the Universe by now and would be planning to return to her house to search for it. Oddly that didn't bother her. Everything was already breaking down; they'd only be speeding up the process. There was nothing she really cared about. She'd be rather sad about her Fancy Beings figurines, but collecting them had only been to while away the hours. Not like her dear new biosphere with its wild assortment of life. Protecting the Universe so it could flourish was a cause worthy of a few broken dolls. A flutter of excitement rushed through her that she hadn't felt for many decades. It had been a while since something meaningful had come her way. What a time!

In a dreamy disposition she lay gazing out the window until her heart thumped upon remembering that she had seen herself on PEACH, sitting in her armchair, playing a game. Odd that this dominated her memory of the brief time there, and not the dark shard that had cut through the bright sky and sent her tumbling and threatened her entire Universe. Another odd thing was she couldn't recall tapping the visor to exit. *What if I'm still inside?* she thought, panicked. *But there are no Gorgons on PEACH. It's based on my DNA and I'm Leffel.*

'Stop worrying about things you know nothing about,' she told herself then tapped her aide on for distraction. She checked news, updates, and notifications, then sent a group message announcing her safe arrival.

With a stretch and yawn, she slid down off a lofty and comfortable bed and went to the window to get a better look outside. In the canopy, air saurs fought over orange fruit and yellow berries, and furry critters swung from branches. The window opened easily when she turned the latch. Sweet melodies rolled in on a fresh, cool breeze that she breathed in while leaning out to look down upon a long garden scattered with fruit trees. At a crick trickling along the forest edge, water saurs dove under the surface plucking at critters with legs, fins, or both, that darted under round tumbling rocks and made the water froth.

Where am I? she wondered. Obviously somewhere in Anon, but little was known about the isolated world. The sky was blue from top to bottom and the light bright and widespread, which meant it was well past her usual waking time. Due to the teleporting time-space difference, they'd left the Domers Club in Equion at dawn and arrived in Anon at around midnight. Exhausted, Gelda hadn't noticed much other than a well-presented and quiet home. She assumed the silence was due to the late hour, but now, despite her late waking, it was still just as quiet, which perhaps accounted for the best sleep she'd had in ages, though being awake for around thirty hours probably had something to do with it.

Her face was greasy from makeup applied a day and a half ago. She felt sweaty and wanted a shower, but the party gown that tugged at her neck and waist was the only clothing she had with her, and she didn't want to have to put it back on afterwards. In the adjoining suite, she used the facilities and assessed the gown in the mirror to see if there was a way of adjusting it for comfort rather than style, but couldn't see how without ruining it. Maybe she could find something else to wear. Tolbert had said something about getting what she needed. Well, she desperately needed a change of clothes. Other than her attire, she decided she didn't look too bad otherwise. Her eyes were as clear as her mind, and she felt no aches or pains. While odd, it was a welcome change from the steadfast lethargy that dictated her days.

Downstairs, she found the house just as silent and empty as upstairs and wondered if she was the first to rise. Stomach rumbling and tongue dry, she wandered from room to room. Despite the stark and minimal furnishings that looked barely used, the house was large and comfortable. In the kitchen, a plain white dining setting appeared wear-and-tear free and a large glass fridger was well stocked. She took a cup from a shelf, filled it with water from a dispenser, gulped it down and then another, then continued to explore. In the lounge four squat armchairs around a large square table looked barely sat on. The only colour in the room were large art pieces of white shapes on brightly coloured backgrounds. There was an office, a media room, and a closed door with the Cosmo Dome symbol on it. She knocked. There was no answer, and she didn't feel right about opening it.

At the back of the house, an open door let in the sound of voices. Gelda went outside and followed a path to Tolbert's workshop. It matched the house in design but not size. Surrounding the entrance were the boxes and equipment Tolbert had left there while searching for the Cosmo Dome equipment before he'd left for Equion. Fortunately, the weather had been good since then.

Expecting the same orderly comfortable sparsity as in the house, Gelda got a rude shock seeing the mess piled almost to the ceiling and filling the room to an impenetrable level. As she stood there considering two routes before her – one narrow and one wide – a gentle and melodic voice startled her.

'Tawawa, guest!' It seemed to come from somewhere above, but looking up revealed nothing but a dirty ceiling.

'Ah, tawawa!' Tolbert appeared at the end of the narrow passageway wearing a leather apron over a faded blue shirt and no shoes.

Gelda met up with him to see a faint blue waveform hovering before him. They exchanged routine small-talk. 'Did you sleep well?' Tolbert asked, to which Gelda replied, 'Yes, thank you. Your house is lovely,' and so on. Neither were particularly comfortable in new company, but they were gracious and experienced enough to know what was expected of them. Helpful information was exchanged and Gelda learnt that they were in the remote High Forest of Merlavin and that the only way in and out of the large property was via the spactor or a flyover. It was a three-day trek by foot up and down steep mountains down into the nearest settlement in the Sandreyik Valley.

Gelda looked around the workshop, paying particular attention to the shelves of broken devices. 'You like to fix things?'

'I do.'

She laughed. 'Then we've met at an opportune moment.' When he gave a curious frown, she explained, 'Most of my household is in a state of disrepair.' She looked around to see if there was someone else with them and found no one. 'Who greeted me when I entered?'

'Ah, that would be SID.' Tolbert's eyes went to the faint blue waveform and he frowned. 'SID?' He got no answer. 'SID, are you there?'

'Oh, so I can speak now?' SID asked in a sulky voice.

Gelda watched the waveform roll up and down to reflect her tone.

Tolbert gave a weary sigh and smile. 'Of course. I asked her to be quiet so I could think,' he told Gelda.

'I already had a solution,' SID said. 'Would you like to know what it is?'

'In a moment, SID. First, I'd like you to meet Gelda, the Universe player. Gelda, meet SID, a superintelligence who helps me process and make decisions.'

'Tawawa, Gelda. You're from outside. I recognised your voice,' said SID. 'It's good to finally be able to converse with you.'

'Tawawa SID. Wait – so you're who Tolbert was speaking to?' Gelda laughed and said to Tolbert, 'I thought it was odd that you keep talking to someone in front of you who wasn't visible. I wondered if it was a consequence of remote living. I did it myself a few lifetimes ago and got into the habit of talking to myself.'

Tolbert laughed along with her. 'I must have seemed odd. Admittedly, I'm out of practice with socialising, but no, I wasn't talking to myself. I would have introduced you, but the system that SID inhabits was in mobile format so access was limited to just me and you wouldn't have seen her waveform either. Anyway, SID started talking to me a few centuries ago through System and we've become best of friends.'

'System granted me permission first,' SID explained. 'I would never barge into an occupied space.'

'SID speaks through the functioning structure,' said Tolbert, 'Or so we believe.'

'We don't really know. Mostly I just observe and report.'

'Fascinating,' said Gelda. 'Are you a function or a discorporate being?'

'All I know for certain is that I'm here.'

Tolbert said, 'She could be an unplanned function or a side-effect of an operational process I adjusted, deleted, or added—'

'Or maybe I was just lonely and wanted a friend, so I became System's consciousness because you were lonely and wanted a friend, too.'

Tolbert laughed, though Gelda wasn't so certain SID meant it to be funny.

'Really, I'm just happy for her company and counsel,' Tolbert continued. 'SID is intuitive, which I am not, and she's also good at finding patterns.'

'Patterns are everything,' said SID.

'You'll get no argument from me. Anyway, she's my System Integration Director and I couldn't do without her.'

'My role is to ensure Tolbert is willingly productive at least eighty percent of the time.'

'Some lives I met the target, some I fell short,' he admitted.

'And this one?' Gelda queried.

Tolbert lightly chuckled. The question would have seemed intrusive coming from someone else, but Gelda's genuine curiosity and warmth made it easy for him to consider and answer it. 'Let's see... It started splendidly with some unforgettable relationships and rewarding inventions, but things turned pear-shaped a few decades ago.'

'Eighty-eight years in and it's fallen short by thirty-seven percent,' SID estimated. 'I blame myself.'

'It would be much worse if you weren't here.' Tolbert smiled softly.

'There's still plenty of time to make this life count,' Gelda assured him while realising her words applied as much to her own, but it was easier to give advice than to accept it.

For a moment there was silence, and then SID said, 'A Universe player! How exciting. I would absolutely love to assist you to play, Gelda, if you would allow me to.'

'How lovely, SID. Thank you.' Gelda noticed Tolbert's code-board. 'Have you found what's causing the glitch?'

He shook his head. 'No, but I can confirm we have one.'

When Tolbert asked, Gelda told him how it had happened.

'Ah, it's how we lost the other twelve Universes.'

Eyes wide, Gelda asked, 'Cats dented them as well?'

Tolbert laughed. 'That would be something! No, they all had a premature initiation and a malfunctioning planet in the construction stage.' Tolbert thought some more. 'It could be a seeding issue...' He pulled up data and indicated several symbols.

'What's that?' Gelda pointed out characters almost identical to the glitching planet code, except split in two with the addition of colons, *P:E AC:H* followed by the same error code 151-34/36. 'That's got to be a clue.'

Tolbert shrugged. 'I've never had to inspect a planet's back-data before. SID, can you shed light on it?'

'It's double-coded,' said SID. 'Coder Initials SS.'

'Shellany,' said Tolbert.

'Yes?' she said appearing behind them. She'd changed out of her checked dress and boots and now wore black leggings and a green tee that matched her eyes and hair streak. Her long black hair was pulled up in a high ponytail that revealed her delicate narrow face and pointed chin. She seemed relaxed and yet alert.

'Ah, there you are,' said Tolbert. 'Tawawa.'

'Tawawa,' said Gelda.

'Tawawa,' Shellany replied in customary sincerity before swiftly taking her attention to the game data on the display behind Tolbert. 'Found anything?' She slipped past her dad to sit in his chair in front of it.

'We were wondering about planet codename PEACH and its double-coded backdata.'

'Oh, that. I did it last night when I couldn't sleep. It was bugging me that I couldn't even get past the planet code to view the stats so I bypassed its security which gave me access to the backdata.' Shellany revealed a separate overlay with rows of data. She tapped away on Tolbert's codeboard, making the data move and change, then returned to the previous overlay with the planet name. 'The trick to deciphering the code is in the second and fifth letters. She typed out the full words of each of the other letters so they could see that 'P' stood for 'Planet' and 'AC' for 'Advanced Civilisation'. She then clicked on the second and fifth letters, 'E' and 'H'.

'I find it's much better to refer to a place and its people by name rather than code,' said Shellany.

'Earth,' read Gelda. The modest planet name evoked plentiful variety. 'Humans.' The term spoke of slow growth but limitless potential. Though the humans of Earth prevented her from finishing her Universe, Gelda found herself feeling affection towards them. Perhaps it had something to do with being there. It was probably more likely due to seeing herself there.

'I saw myself there,' she blurted, causing them both to frown.

'You mean metaphorically or someone who looked like you?'

Tolbert asked after a pause.

'The Universe is based on your DNA so that's entirely possible,' said Shellany.

Gelda shook her head. 'I don't mean someone like me. It was *me* in *my* house with *my* friends, playing a game that was probably this one.'

'Are you sure?'

She closed her eyes and clearly saw herself sitting in her armchair. 'Yes.' Silence followed. Gelda waited for someone to say something. No one did. 'How is that possible? Is it part of the Universe glitch?'

Shellany and Tolbert looked at each another. Neither said anything.

'What?' probed Gelda. 'Tell me.'

They seemed to come to a silent arrangement about who should speak. Tolbert won out. 'You know that a glitch destroyed the other twelve Universes?'

'Um, yes. You told me roughly ten minutes ago.'

'Of course. Well, before those Universes died, we contacted each player, and they all said the same thing.'

'That they saw themselves inside? That's unbelievable! What else did they say? Is there any way I can speak with them?'

Tolbert nodded.

'Tell her,' Shellany prodded her father.

'It wasn't just their Universes that died. They died, too.'

TWENTY-TWO
One Toy Only

A long teeth-shattering screech shattered the silence in the empty streets of Alkupera Town as Ludor yanked the steering wheel hard into a row of parked cars, scraping side to side until one locked with his. Pushing the locked car against the ones ahead, he revved harder until a gap formed, then reverse parked into it with a *thunk!* as he hit the car behind.

'Wrong street, arsehole,' Debrov muttered from the backseat just loud enough for Ludor to hear.

Ludor didn't bother replying but pointed above a yellow building across the street to a sign between two four-storey windows. It read, 'Domers Club' with an arrow pointing down an alley.

They headed across the road in threes. With Mutt on a leash, Ludor took FORCE and BRISK, then Debrov waited five minutes before following him with FIERCE and SHARP. Though the day was barely over, this evening it seemed the townsfolk were having an early one.

'Don'ts anyone party around here?' said BRISK.

'Leffels are a buncho boring farks,' replied FIERCE.

They encountered no one all the way to the Domers Club door. With a single kick, FORCE brought it down and in they went. Ludor tied Mutt to a wooden column where he flopped to the floor, sad-eyed, tail thumping. Resisting a playful roughing up of the amiable hound, Ludor looked around.

Debrov wandered around the room. 'So much treasure to trash.' Overwhelmed by choice, her eyes travelled across shelves of books, trophies, and framed photographs that lined the foyer walls.

'Plenty some good clean stuff to fark up.' FIERCE almost drooled at the prospect of trashing the place.

'Agreed,' agreed BRISK.

'Leave nothing standing' Debrov swiped a hand across a shelf, bringing paraphernalia crashing down.

The trievers took it as permission to get into some prime farkery. Down came shelves. Over went bookcases. Through went fists and weapons.

Ludor was more interested in a closed door with light coming out from under it. He got FORCE to kick it in, but it was sturdier than the outside door. FIERCE and BRISK lent a hand and down it crashed. Captain and trievers in trail, in he went.

Behind the partition wall, the Domers sat in the rest area with their packs packed waiting for Shellany to collect them. Lanseth had sent several messages that showed as unsent on his aide. Upon hearing crashing noises in the foyer, he'd sent another: *Gorgons are here! Come now but be careful. Tawawa!*

The Gorgons sauntered in. The trievers broke away from their bosses and wandered around picking up and dropping stuff, then kicking it if it didn't break. FORCE and FIERCE bashed their weapons against the partition wall until there was more of it down than up, revealing the Domers standing behind the low table, chairs discarded.

'There's nothing here you want,' Lanseth said as Ludor and Debrov stepped over the rubble towards them.

'Is that so?' Debrov stealthily approached and weighed up the situation: weakling Leffels, no weapons, full packs. 'Shall I interrogate them?' she asked Ludor.

Ludor did his own weighing up. The full packs confirmed they'd been expecting them, which meant they knew something and had probably devised an annoying time-consuming obstacle between him and delivering the toy to Boss King. In reply to Debrov's question, he shook his head. 'Bring me anything that looks... Domey.' They knew what they were after.

The trievers blasted into action. They opened doors to cupboards and rooms and destroyed anything that didn't resemble the target item. Ludor noted the empty locker cabinets under the window, then signalled to Debrov to do her thing. Getting close to their faces, she circled the Domers. 'Where are you going with those packs?' The farkery on her mind was evident in her grin as she toyed with them. Without warning, she yanked Lanseth's off his back and tore it open. Out spilled cords, controllers, a bunch of small devices, and his check-patterned capsule. She shoved a hand inside it and pulled out his Essaverse.

'Found it!' She held it up.

'Careful! That's fragile!' Lanseth warned.

'What, this?' Debrov tossed it from hand to hand.

Snatching it from her, Ludor opened the capsule and tipped out the four balls inside. The biosphere was black, blue, and white. 'It's not the Universe.' When he let go of it, Lanseth's Essaverse hit the floor with a clunk.

'Careful!' said all of the Domers at once.

'What the actual fark?' Debrov yanked the packs off the rest of the Domers' backs and tipped out each capsule. 'Is this some kind of decoy?'

'It's a collection,' Ludor said wearily. 'There's six of them in total.'

'I count six here, so one of them must be the Universe.'

'I have two,' Prinn confessed then quickly shut her mouth.

'Nice try,' said Debrov. 'Which one is the Universe?'

'We don't have one. I have an Essaverse,' said Lanseth.

'And I have a Thalverse,' said Alrick right afterwards.

Renoy shook his head and sighed. 'There's a Bonverse in mine.'

Prinn said woefully. 'Mine has my two Wellaverses. Please don't hurt them.'

Debrov chortled. 'I think we can all agree that some prime farkery is going to happen to your precious toys. I tell you what: if you release the Universe, we'll limit the disfigure-ments to your arms and legs and leave your pretty little Leffel faces alone.'

Renoy scoffed. 'You'd fark us up even if we had it.'

Debrov laughed. 'So true. I have little control over the squad once they're in a frenzy. Hand over the toy and I'll stop them before they maim you for life.'

The trievers returned empty-handed.

'Nothing worth nothing,' said SHARP.

'Ramp up farkery?' FIERCE asked.

Ludor ignored them and emptied the coloured balls s from the remaining cannisters. He studied them long and hard. None of them resembled Boss King's image. He'd been right. They were all a little different and the Universe was far more complex looking. 'It's not here,' he concluded.

'Smash them?' said Debrov.

Ludor gave them the go ahead.

As FORCE raised a sledgehammer over his head, Renoy said quickly but calmly, 'Pretty sure Boss King will fark you up if you destroy them.'

Debrov pressed her face against his. 'What the fark do you know?'

Despite her rotten breath, Renoy didn't flinch. 'Not a lot, but I figure he'd want them for his collection.'

'He only wants the Universe,' Ludor stated plainly.

'Two collections are better than one,' Renoy said with a casual shrug.

Lanseth caught on to Alrick's ruse and exclaimed in fake shock, 'Stop encouraging them to take our Cosmo Domes!'

Alrick played a more realistic hand. 'He might as well have them. Least they'll be looked after.' Severing their biospheres was far from looking after them, but if the Gorgons took them, they would at least have time to figure out how to get them back.

Debrov looked to Ludor and shrugged. 'Could mean extra barrels.' Boss King often threw in barrels of brew as rewards for good work.

'Or bonus pay,' said SHARP.

'Extra free times,' was BRISK's vote.

Ludor thought on it briefly. If left to the trievers, they would probably end up accidentally breaking the additional toys on the way back. They weren't exactly careful with their weaponry. As for Debrov, she had a weakness for smashing things when told not to. That all meant the responsibility would fall to him, as usual. He was done with this task even before it began, and he didn't need more responsibilities and diversions. 'We're here for one toy and that's what we're leaving with. Smash them.'

'No!' Prinn rushed at the loose balls containing equipment and chambered biospheres, gathered them in her arms, and knelt with them under her torso.

FIERCE laughed and raised her sledgehammer. Lanseth only just managed to drag Prinn away before it came down. A single blow got two capsules. Chips and dents appeared in their preservation chambers as they rolled unevenly away. It took a few more bashes before black shards of rock flew into the air and the Cosmo Domes cracked open. The biospheres inside instantly turned to dust.

'You destroyed them!' Prinn sobbed.

Alrick rushed at FORCE to stop her smashing more, but BRISK pushed him to the ground before he got there. Renoy attempted to reclaim three chambers that rolled away, but SHARP kicked his legs from underneath him. FORCE resumed an attack, and with a grunt, smashed a few more chambers to smithereens with a pickaxe. With the Domers watching on in shock, the other trievers finished them off. When they were done, there was nothing left but crushed rock, dust, and a sweet metallic smell.

Ludor observed the carnage with interest and found it curious how the four Domers huddled together consoling each other. No one in Dirt City cared enough to get upset about anything, and here were four people comforting each other over a few broken toys. He didn't understand it at all, and he didn't like the tight feeling it gave him in the chest when Debrov toyed with them, drawing mild blood, small fractures, and gentle cries.

Debrov leapt at Lanseth, locking him in a wide-eyed stare, knife to throat. 'Where's the toy?'

'I told you. It's not here,' Lanseth replied through tight lips.

'One last chance before we cut loose.'

Lanseth said nothing.

Ludor watched on without giving anything away. He found it unsettling that the Domers just sat there instead of fighting back. In Gorgonia, refusing to brawl brought shame and showed weakness. Perhaps it showed strength here. While only a theory, it made him mad that they might consider themselves superior. While he loathed the Gorgon life, Leffels were still the enemy. When Debrov looked over for his command, he nodded. 'Take them down.'

TWENTY-THREE
Inside Job

In the full shine of noon, the gardens of Tolbert's cloud forest estate were vibrant with noise and colour. Trees and grounds were alive with land and air critters, while fleurs opened to let in light and air and give out colour and fragrance. Gelda took a moment to appreciate the lovely chaos. Needing a moment alone, she had left the workshop after offering to grab extra chairs from the house. Now she sat on a garden seat and sighed. It was a nice place to sit and think, but it didn't stop her worries for long.

It wasn't just their Universes that died. They died, too.

The discussion after Tolbert's bombshell left her reeling. Dying was such a strange and portentous concept with frightening connotations. It made her queasy. Life was ongoing, that's just the way it was. Until it wasn't. Until now. Her options looped, except they weren't valid options at all.

She would stop playing. Easy.

Not so easy. Then everyone inside her Universe would die. They're mortal; they'll die anyway. But the whole biosphere would die if she stopped playing. It's a complete organism. Pieces of it die so that life goes on. Those pieces are people and one of those people is me. I will die.

She wouldn't stop playing. Easy.

She would save the Universe, and herself.

Back in the workshop Shellany and Tolbert discussed how to fix the glitch, searching for a pattern in a sea of randomness.

'I blame myself,' Shellany said when Gelda returned. 'I was so worried about the Gorgons, that I rushed you through construction. I didn't think about the consequences of Divine Intervention mode. I didn't think about the...'

'Dying thing?'

'Yes, that.'

'I'm still going to play.'

'That's brave of you.' Tolbert awkwardly patted her on the back.

'You've only got one life left,' Shellany reminded her. 'In the game, I mean.'

'And for real, if I lose it.' Gelda laughed. 'But one life's all I need, right? One final rebirth.'

Shellany gave a nervous laugh. 'Absolutely. You're an excellent player,' Shellany assured her. 'And this is all moot if we fix the glitch.' Shellany pressed keys on the codeboard. 'Some good and bad news. The good news is that the evolution accelerator increased the humans to 89% advancement, and the time scale gauge now sits on the cusp of Eternity. The bad news is it's still not enough for Earth to qualify as prime.'

An overlay with lines of symbols appeared on a small display in the cramped workspace in front of them. 'We could keep patching it with subquests, sidequests, minigames, and other minor code alterations. It will probably crawl forward and maybe reach the mark, but that's only avoiding the real problem, which is the hole caused by the fall. That's where we need to focus our attention.'

Father and daughter studied the symbols for quite some time.

Tolbert said, 'We could add a storyline.'

'Make it mortal-driven?' Shellany suggested.

'An inside job. I like it!' Tolbert leaned over her to evaluate the data.

'It has to be part of the gameplay.' Shellany tried to expand the display so they could read the stats and see precisely what was happening, but there wasn't room. She eyed up the boxes and paraphernalia. 'How can you work like this, Dad? You really need to clear this place out.' She tried pushing boxes out of the way, but nothing budged. She rubbed her hands together to remove dust and dirt.

'It took me half a day just to make a path to retrieve the mainframe and control panel, and that was with robot help,' Tolbert said defensively.

'Granted, you wasted time trying to do it yourself before you conceded to the house robot,' SID remarked.

'I'm surprised you can find anything,' Gelda said.

'He keeps what's important to him nearby,' said SID.

'Not everything.' Shellany raised an eyebrow and shot a glance at her father.

Tolbert looked away and his face grew serious.

Gelda broke the awkward moment by looking around and saying, 'This isn't ideal. Surely the bare essentials to playing any game well are comfortable seating and clean... space?'

Shellany nodded in full agreement. 'Exactly. You'll play in the comfort of the gaming room. Help me move everything into the house.'

Tolbert's blank face turned horrified. 'What? No! System has never been moved! There are too many unknown factors that could make it unstable!'

'The house?' SID said quietly, as though the mysterious place was entirely fictional.

To the shock of her father, Shellany detached the control panel from the mainframe and put them in the satchel along with the codeboard. 'It's happening,' was all she said as she slung the satchel over her shoulder and headed out the door.

'Bring that back!' Tolbert yelled with little authority.

Gelda wondered what it was between them that caused him to behave remorsefully. She followed Shellany into the house and found her in the room that had been closed previously.

'Is this a gaming room?' It was a place like none other.

'It seems so.' Shellany arranged equipment on a round table in the centre of six gaming stations. Each station was shaped like a quarter dome with a flat bottom and curved top that opened to a semicircle. High-back, cushioned white chairs were at the entrance of each, with the name of the Cosmo Dome model on the back and rows of controls on the arms.

Gelda swivelled around the one labelled 'Universe' so she

could see inside its station. A contoured table framed the lower half with a squat round podium in the middle. The rest of the space seemed dedicated to the display – or at least she hoped so.

While Shellany hooked up the codeboard to the control panel, Gelda tested the Universe chair. When she sat, it automatically contoured perfectly to her height and shape.

SID sounded relieved when Shellany switched System on. Her waveform flowed in long soft curves of green. 'It's much nicer in here than the workshop. I guess change isn't so bad.'

Gelda swivelled the chair round to face Shellany, though it was SID she addressed. 'Can you see?'

'Not the way you can. I sense the atmosphere of a space, and this one is soft and quiet. I'm guessing it's neat?'

The women laughed.

'It is,' Shellany confirmed.

Gelda thought it odd that Tolbert hadn't yet appeared, but Shellany brought her attention back by saying, 'We really must get you something more comfortable to wear.' She looked her up and down. 'What's your preferred ensemble and size?' After Gelda told her, Shellany pressed buttons on her aide. A simulated command panel appeared before her, and a column of virtual coloured strands emerged from the ground between them. 'The connection to the fabric store is pretty poor, but hopefully it will access enough material for our needs.'

'What is that thing?'

'It's a made-to-fit virtual weaving loom. Let's make you something to play in.'

Shellany accessed the apparel fabric section on the panel, then asked for Gelda's preferences in fabrics, styles, and colours. Gelda chose comfortable, neutral underwear, and trousers in dark grey and light grey pinstripes.

Shellany made the selection. 'Simple and elegant. Top style and colour?'

Gelda thought for a moment. 'Something billowy. I'm rarely brave enough to wear yellow. Not bright yellow, golden.' She thought some more. 'Make it floral. Put tiny white random fleurs all over it.'

'There's one here that says, "Fresh and Crisp"?' Shellany offered and showed her a picture.

Gelda smiled and nodded. 'It's almost exactly how I pictured it.'

Gelda took off her gown and stood still on Shellany's command while she accessed the loom. The virtual column of coloured strands moved to surround Gelda and fit her shape.

'It will only take a few minutes,' Shellany said then left to go find Tolbert.

The loom whirred busily away, and the strands grew more tangible as they fashioned the outfit. The moving thread brushed against Gelda's skin as it was woven. When done, the new garments fit snuggly without being too tight. It was good to be out of the gown. She went into the bathroom to see how it looked and decided the style suited her. 'I look great!' she murmured. Downstairs, she heard voices in the kitchen. She tried not to listen in, but the words echoed through the house.

'Giorana knew you were my dad,' she heard Shellany say. 'She convinced me it was a chance for me to get back at you for abandoning us.'

So that's it, thought Gelda. Seems this is getting sorted before playing, not after. Probably for the best.

'I didn't abandon you, love,' said Tolbert. 'I just didn't know how else to protect you.'

'What I don't understand is how you could move to such a wonderful place and leave your family behind! You should have brought us with you.'

'To the middle of nowhere away from friends and community? I couldn't do that to you.'

'You didn't give me the choice.'

'I'm sorry. I thought it was the right thing to do.'

'How could you think such a thing?' Silence ran deep for a moment, then Shellany softened her tone. 'Giorana assumed I hated you enough to go through with the theft, but it only proved I don't. I guess that's something.'

'That is something,' Tolbert replied.

Gelda waited for him to apologise in a more meaningful manner, to say something that would trigger an open discussion, but the conversation faded. In the silence that followed, Gelda entered the room. On the kitchen bench was a bowl of juicy plumkins on a bed of greeneries. Next to it, a serving tray held tart flanthies with fragrant floralnuts and a bowl of whipped caora butter.

Shellany looked up from the stove where she was brewing jova and squealed with delight. 'You look simply wonderful!' She went over and circled Gelda. 'Are you comfortable?'

'It's like wearing air.' Gelda laughed. 'You must connect me to the store.'

Shellany tapped away on her aide while Tolbert took a loaf of freshly baked bredde from the oven. It released a steamy, savoury aroma when he sliced it. 'I thought we could share a nourishing breakfast to see us through what will likely be a long and exhaustive process.' He arranged pieces on the tray with the flanthies.

'Looks delicious. Thank you.' Gelda smeared caora butter on a flanthie and took a plumkin and a handful of floral nuts to have with it. They ate on the deck overlooking the forest. As she sipped the rich and smooth jova, she thought how lovely it was in the cloud forest. The mountain air really was something.

They topped up their jovas and took them into the gaming room. When Tolbert busied himself adjusting the lighting and sound on the gaming system, it seemed to Gelda as if he was unfamiliar with it all. 'Haven't played in a while then?' she said, hoping to perhaps learn more about her host who didn't speak much.

'I've never played in here,' he confessed while fiddling with the room's airflow.

'Really? Why?'

'He gave up playing Cosmo Dome after the Gorgon attack,' said SID.

Tolbert's sinking body and lowered face spoke loudly about sadness.

'You set up the room when you moved here then?' Shellany asked.

Tolbert's nod was slightly less disheartened but still melancholy.

Gelda cautiously prodded for more. 'Which means you *wanted* to play.'

Tolbert straightened and looked over. 'Somewhat. I'm an inventor more than a player, which makes it hard to enjoy playing as I'm always looking for faults.'

'You want it to be perfect.' Gelda understood.

'And nothing is perfect,' they said in unison and laughed.

'It's silly, I know, but I had the perfect gaming room design in mind for Cosmo Dome, and I just had to get it out. I had the time and the will and made it happen. I didn't think much about it getting used as I'm used to being alone, but I come in here now and then to imagine if that ever happened.' He smiled at Gelda when he said that. 'I never quite believed that someone would ever come to my secluded home to play my favourite game invention – and yet here we are.'

'Yes, we are,' agreed Gelda. Seeing each station fully equipped with an active biosphere hooked up and flourishing would be quite something.

'Let's fix this glitch and save the Universe!' Shellany proposed. She opened the capsule, took the Cosmo Dome out, and positioned it on the podium inside its allocated station. She then set up the mainframe console and equipment. Instead of switching it on, she cabled it to the central station. A wave of blue energy travelled from the mainframe to the central control.

Without asking or waiting for an invitation, Shellany dragged the chair up to the central station and pulled the console and codeboard towards her. Silently focussed, she pressed buttons. The display appeared, and she scrolled up and down while Tolbert wandered off to think.

'You seem to know what you're doing,' Gelda remarked.

'It's how we used to do it when we were colleagues,' Shellany revealed. 'He would devise the broad idea, I'd test the code, we both knuckled the details out. He would assemble, we both tested, he directed, and I steered.'

'How cooperative.' Gelda was happy to see a reconciliation begin.

'Shellany understands Cosmo Dome almost as well as I do,' Tolbert called out from near the door. 'She brought Help to life,' he added with pride.

'Such talent!' Gelda laughed. 'Whose idea was it to add the upsells?'

'Ah, those.' Tolbert looked sheepish. 'I hired an aggressive marketing company. They were targeting inventors and lured me in with a free toolbox that wasn't available anywhere else.'

'They were certainly something,' said Gelda.

'If by something you mean confounding,' he agreed. 'They're the reason why there's branding plastered on the overlays. For the lives of me, I haven't been able to remove them.'

The central display gave them full access to all Cosmo Dome activity via System. With Tolbert's help, Gelda hooked the Universe up to it and pressed the *Start* button. The game appeared in program mode.

'To ensure overall sustainability of your Universe biosphere, please select a suitable prime for this galaxy,' Help began again on repeat.

Tolbert muted the audio so they could focus on the issue at hand.

'There is a high probability that I can reroute CD-Help.'

'Thank you, SID, but we don't need administration right now,' Tolbert said.

Shellany experimented with a few workarounds involving the planet codename PAACU. Its backdata revealed its official name was Andrilon and its people were Urlins. 'At 96% suitability, Andrilon is the next eligible planet to oversee the galaxy as prime.' Shellany attempted to set Earth as dysfunctional to force the system to approve Andrilon as a delegate, but it failed. 'The game system refuses to let me set Earth as dysfunctional.'

A new message appeared in the view: There was an error due to the Cosmo Dome features configuration process. Your original configuration will be restored. 'OK'.

Shellany tried forcing the decision by hacking the disabled function only to get another warning message: Any attempt to continue play without assigning a solution will result in imminent immobilisation. Cause: civilisation error.

She clicked on the small lightbulb icon under the message and read the pop-up description. 'System-suggested solutions. Worth a try.' There were five options:

- Disease
- Ice Age
- Extraterrestrial intervention
- Civilisation overhaul
- Reset planet data

'Definitely no to resetting the data, and disease has too many unknown variables,' said Tolbert.

'An ice age would take too long,' said Shellany. 'What about a civilisation overhaul?'

'System's calculations determine there is a 31% chance of success that a civilisation overhaul would reach the desired outcome,' said SID when asked.

'Counts that out. Extraterrestrial intervention could work,' said Shellany. 'We could get someone from a qualifying civilisation to perform a quest to execute the changes.'

'Except that option is greyed out. You abandoned that sequence, remember?' SID reminded Tolbert.

'Yes, we decided it was being overcautious,' said Tolbert.

'It wouldn't take long to rewrite,' said Shellany. 'We could even customise it to be planet-specific.'

Tolbert chuckled. 'I forgot how much you love coding.'

'It's the source of everything,' Shellany claimed.

'Wrong. Patterns are,' SID disputed.

'Depends on your reality.'

'Speaking of realities, maybe one day when you're not too busy doing system-related activities, you'll be interested to hear my solution.'

'What solution?' Tolbert ignored her tone. SID rarely meant to come across as contrary or patronising.

'The one I was about to tell you about in the workshop before you paused me.'

'The solution please, SID. A reminder of the initial problem would be nice, too.'

'Of course. The problem is that CD-Help is constrained by the perimeters of the game. That limits player decision-making so we cannot be certain that the choices presented are the only ones available.'

'That is true. And the solution?' asked Tolbert.

'Me.'

'You?'

'Correct,' said SID. 'I integrate with CD-Help like I do with System so we coexist as three coequal entities sharing one structure to deliver consistent administration. System provides processing and CD-Help game functionality, and I hold it all together as decoder, director, and personality because System is just System and CD-Help could do with one.'

'Oh, but I quite like her,' Gelda remarked. 'She's so polite.'

'She will still be present though improved.'

'A SID-influenced version you mean?' Tolbert joked.

'Precisely. What do you say?'

They discussed it and decided it made sense to have a combined administrator and processor in charge. Decision made, the three non-biological entities went quiet for a brief moment.

'Tawawa, friends. I am the voice of System, Help, and SID. We have bonded and are so far getting along nicely and don't anticipate any issues. Obeying your will and command in accordance with established rules and regulations is our sole undertaking. All instructions, advice, warnings, and general banter will be relayed via The All-knowing Voice that you can change in Settings if you prefer a different tone. We are here to operate and assist you in all of your daily activities, including the current Cosmo Dome project of saving the Universe biosphere. Please assign a name that reflects the three of us.'

After a brief discussion they decided that since technically SID was a title, it still applied. The newly-formed triple entity agreed. With the new and improved SID instructing via The All-knowing Voice, which they didn't change, they then got to writing a sequence to fix the glitch. Symbols and numbers in chaotic and neat patterns flowed across and down the display as Shellany shuffled them around, added or deleted single characters or entire rows, and created new patterns.

Gelda watched for a moment then asked what she could do.

'Rest up. You'll need energy for when you play,' said Tolbert.

'I have plenty of energy.' It was surprising how sprite and motivated she was. It was also good to be out of the house and not have things breaking all around her, other than the Universe glitch.

'You could play minigames to earn coins,' said Shellany. 'Can we enable dual input on this setup?' she asked Tolbert.

'It won't affect the programming, and a full bounty will come in handy.'

'For what?' Gelda wondered.

'I'm not sure yet.' Tolbert altered some settings. The band of muted colour around the Universe station brightened as its projection appeared on the screen within.

Gelda sat back in the chair and inspected the features of her station. The display went all around and over her head for total immersive play. There was a stocked snack cabinet with cooling and heating devices under one side of the table. She pressed buttons on the chair arms to see what they did. One made windows slide open at head level on either side of the chair. There were several speakers. One had buttons next to it with each Cosmo Dome model on them.

Shellany answered questions, then showed Gelda how to access the main menu and what the buttons, icons, and sub-menus did. When Gelda was confident enough to go solo, she assured Shellany she was okay. After Shellany returned to her coding, Gelda clicked through to the *Minigames* menu appeared at the bottom left of the display. There were three choices: Match Three, Hidden Objects, or Shoot-up. The stats revealed the shoot-up had the best chance of earning coins fast, so she got comfortable in the game seat and shot at meteors. Exploding them was fun and she quickly got good at it. When the coin indicator read 999,999,999 it flashed in an ultra-bold font that sparkled and fizzed. The last meteor she hit exploded in a colourful blast of three-dimensional shapes.

'Yes!' she whispered excitedly and turned to share her achievements. Tolbert and Shellany were engaged in a deep discission about a new mode that would give the player more influence, which apparently was challenging when limited by the game perimeters. It was lovely to see them getting along and working as a team, and they seemed to be getting somewhere, so she left them to it. While resting was prob-ably a wise move (at home she would be taking a nap about now), Gelda played the hidden objects minigame instead, then the match three and a few others. The stats revealed top earnings with unlimited autocorrects, some intriguing equipment and tools, and powerups that granted play in a variety of modes, some for a limited time and others limited situations. She thought about having a rest or a snack, something to keep her going but realised she felt fine.

While Gelda played minigames, Tolbert and Shellany had an in-depth discussion about the hole on Earth caused by Finkle knocking the biosphere off the bench and agreed that it was the glitch.

Tolbert said, 'I think I may have figured out what's going on. Out here, we see a dent but inside, it's a ruptured space-time continuum. The outside is seeping in and the inside is seeping out to cause a cosmic fracture.'

'They're merging,' Shellany concluded.

'Exactly.'

'It sounds serious,' replied Gelda. 'How do we fix it?'

Tolbert shrugged. 'It's a hole. We plug it.'

'Right. How?'

'We squeeze some kind of cosmic filler into it,' said Shellany.

Gelda laughed. 'You're talking metaphorically, right?'

'Kind of. We would need to add another subquest.'

'That's no small task.' Tolbert wandered to think. 'Let's return to the mortal-driven storyline,' he said after a while. 'What if we got someone on the inside to patch the hole from the ground up.'

'A human wouldn't be up to the task. It would have to be someone from another planet.'

'Andrilon,' said Gelda.

'Yes, Andrilon. An Urlin.'

They discussed it some more and came up with a gameplan. Shellany added and shuffled around more code. Symbols flashed, glyphs shifted. Tolbert made suggestions. Shellany added and shuffled some more.

'That's it!' said Tolbert after a while. 'Good work! Let's integrate it.'

Shellany punched at more buttons. A great quantity of code filled the central display in tightly-crammed rows. Symbols shifted sideways or swapped places, lines scrolled and phrases lit up, dulled, or disappeared as she silently toiled. Space began to appear at the bottom of the display. It lifted until all code vanished except one line. Shellany thought for a moment then quickly added more code.

Finally, she sank back into her chair. 'Done!'

'It worked?' Gelda asked.

All that was left on the display was a flashing diamond in the centre and a single query: *A storyline is detected. Code new nested levels, Remind me later, Cancel.*

'System willingly and thankfully consents to the new storyline,' said SID. 'Way to go, team.'

'We have our quest!' They high-fived.

Gelda wanted to ask what they had done but knew she wouldn't understand the technical details. When ready, they would tell her in gameplay terms. Tolbert defaulted back to worrying. He hunched over, deep in thought.

'Stop stressing, Dad. It'll work.'

'Tell that to your fingers,' Tolbert retorted.

Shellany's fingers tapped against the table. It's not the bio-sphere that worries me.' Her aide showed several greyed-out messages. 'They're to Lanseth. They won't send.'

'The same happened to me,' Gelda said. 'I sent several messages when I awoke, but none have gone through.' The faulty aide was somewhat to blame but even accessing notifications manually didn't work.

'System reports erratic reception,' SID informed.

'Which means messages get through but not right away,' Tolbert said. 'Reception is often unstable here.'

Shellany tried letting it go but couldn't. 'I've got a feeling I should go back.'

'Not now! You have new levels to write for the subquest.' Tolbert realized he was being insensitive. 'Are you worried for them?'

Shellany nodded. 'The Gorgons might have found them.'

'I'll go,' said Gelda.

'To the clubhouse?' Tolbert wanted to confirm that she understood the nature of the task.

'Yes,' she insisted, sitting up with her getting-things-done smile on. 'You both need to write the new subquest, which leaves me.'

'It's the perfect solution,' agreed Shellany.

'But there might be Gorgons!' Tolbert worried.

'Then wish me well!' Gelda put out her hand for the spactor.

Tolbert didn't move.

'Dad,' said Shellany.

'No. I can't have anyone else harmed over this pesky invention. I'm calling the peacemakers.' He jabbed at his aide.

'You're just worrying!' said Shellany. 'It's a good plan.'

'And if it doesn't go to plan, then things will work themselves out,' Gelda added. She stared encouragingly into his eyes then gently put a hand over his aide. When she put out her hand for the spactor, he hesitated only briefly before surrendering it. 'This is the right thing to do,' she assured him.

After Shellany pointed out its controls, Gelda strapped on the spactor and switched it on. It bleeped. No one spoke while they waited.

'This way is open,' the spactor said finally.

Gelda looked up to see them staring at her, then down to see the rings fully charged.

Shellany grabbed Gelda's shoulders and looked in her eyes. 'You've got this.'

Gelda's heart skipped a beat as she held her gaze. Shellany's confidence in her was absolutely contagious. 'I've got this.'

'Tawawa!' said Shellany with genuine enthusiasm.

'Tawawa!' said Tolbert with genuine effort.

'Tawawa!' With the prospect of encountering all manner of disaster or nothing more than expectant Domers ahead,

Gelda took a deep breath and stepped through.

TWENTY-FOUR
Mutt Chooses

While the trievers enjoyed some prime farkery at the Domers' expense, Ludor returned to the foyer. He wanted to take another look around by himself. When he arrived, Mutt waggled his entire body and stretched the chain tight trying to get to his new friend. The chain shorted, and the column creaked as he zoomed around it.

'Such a mad boy!' Ludor cooed while he untangled the chain. He roughed him up a little and couldn't resist kissing the crown of his head when Mutt pressed close for cuddles. 'Sit,' he said but the good boy was too overcome from attention. 'Sit!' Ludor said in a more commanding voice. Mutt sat but got right back up again. Ludor chuckled. The hound made him feel good, but having feelings was weird and scary and made you vulnerable, just like playfulness and innocence led to beatings.

Leaving the hound chained, Ludor expanded his senses to the corners of the room. Whatever had got his hackles up wasn't here. To a soundtrack of thuds, crashes, groans, and cries from inside the club room, he scavenged through the mess left from the squad's farkery, searching for the toy. It was unlikely to be found, but he couldn't shake a feeling that he was missing something. Leffels fought with their heads using scruples and kindness. It was unfamiliar battle territory, but he had more of a mind than most of his kind. While the cause of his unease eluded him, the prospect of a new challenge brought excitement.

A rhythmic clunking from outside alerted him to someone heading up the stairs. The blood transceiver behind his ear tingled, as it often did when a threat was near. Typically, during a brawl, he would greet a newcomer with his fists, but instinct had him searching for a place to hide. The only place large enough to fit was the one item still standing and intact in the foyer. It was a heavy metal wardrobe bolted to the wall near the door. He yanked it open, tossed out coats, and got inside. Leaving it a fraction open, he watched a Leffel roll a barrel into the building. He recognised Gelda as the one at the house who'd foolishly declared that the toy wasn't yet built. Her arrival was concerning enough, but a barrel? He wondered if she had the toy.

He watched her look nervously around. When her eyes reached the wardrobe, she frowned and took a step towards it, but then noticed Mutt chained to the column. She steadied the barrel on its end then cautiously approach Mutt.

'Tawawa, boy!' she murmured soothingly.

Mutt responded with paws in the air and tongue lolling. When loud and angry voices boomed out from the rest area, her head turned towards the smashed-down door into the club's main room. She looked to the distance a moment then rummaged through her pack. From a small bag she took small pink and yellow treats that she fed to the hound. Fizzling foam formed at the sides of his large mouth as he wolfed them down.

After a scratch behind the ears, Gelda untied him. 'We're friends now so let's protect each other.'

The hound responded with a more vigorous tail wag.

Ludor gritted his teeth. Unlike Gorgons who acted first then suffered the consequences, Leffels were known to think before acting. Fed treats, the hound would prove a worthy ally. He would have to approach this carefully.

The barrel pushed back on its side, Gelda rolled it towards the club rooms with Mutt bounding after her. Ludor crept out of the wardrobe and pressed himself against the club room wall. 'You got a dog? That's so great!' he heard her say with phony cheeriness. 'You're never going to believe what just happened! I was gifted a barrel of top shelf elixir! Who wants some?'

In the silence that followed, Ludor traced her passage into the room and waited behind the only piece of the partition wall left. It offered a good view through a punch hole. Debrov and the trievers held weapons dripping in blood. It appeared they'd just finished brawling when Gelda appeared. Scattered on the floor around them were the Leffels.

With the barrel and everything else forgotten, Gelda cried out, 'Get away from my friends!'

As she bolted towards them with Mutt close behind, Ludor wondered what it would be like to feel something for people other than contempt. He even tried to replicate Gelda's genuine dismay but, no, nothing. It was all just mess and details: broken limbs on feeble unconscious bodies lying on the floor amongst broken stuff.

Gelda didn't get very far before FORCE blocked her. Behind the burly giant, Prinn lay with one arm at a wrong angle and the other pressed against her stomach where a widening patch of blood stained her shirt. Next to her, Alrick was missing an ear and cradling crushed fingers. With a black eye and swollen leg, Renoy sprayed blood from several tiny perforations across the floor. Lanseth was bruised up with a swollen jaw and had blood gushing from a neck wound. The trievers had done a thorough job. Unaccustomed to frequent violence, Leffels fell quickly and took time getting up. They would need to rehabilitate before resuming their lives.

When FORCE wasn't looking, she tried again, but FIERCE picked her up and threw her back across the room where she smacked her head against the barrel, fell, and didn't get up again.

Mutt growled at FORCE who kicked him hard. The pitiful hound yelped then skulked off, tail between his legs, to whimper in a corner.

Leaving his lurking spot, Ludor went to the hound. 'You have to fight back,' he said, comforting him, then approached Gelda.

Hand to head, she sat up. Before she could get to her feet, he towered over her. 'Turn out your pockets and empty your pack.'

Debrov appeared next to him, giving Gelda a cursory glance before standing the barrel on its end. 'Top shelf elixir, you say?'

'It's for my friends.'

'Then consider us friends,' said Debrov. 'BRISK, find some drinkware.'

'There's no time for elixir,' Ludor told her.

Debrov laughed hard. 'There's always time for elixir.'

Enticed by the prospect of elixir the trievers whooped and cheered.

'FORCE, frisk her,' Ludor commanded.

Conflicted, FORCE looked from Gelda to the barrel. It was an easy choice. He lugged the barrel on a broad shoulder into the kitchen. Dragging their bloodied weapons, the other trievers followed him. The squad wouldn't be steered away from the worst elixir let alone the best. They gathered around the barrel. FIERCE poured the heady liquid into whatever would hold it, without bothering to close the valve between pours. Amber liquid splashed on the floor. Mugs were filled and refilled as the retrieval squad took a break from their labours.

Eyes going from the squad to the Leffels, Ludor sighed. He didn't bother to stop Gelda when she hurried over to check on her friends. His will to suffer life was diminishing. Lacking an opinion on the matter, he watched her rip up her shirt and press pieces to wounds, pull an arm back into place, and wrap a missing ear that would either need be reattached or else another would form in a few days with clean gauze and the right medicine.

'This shit is fiery as all fark,' said Debrov as she poured another elixir and gave a wince as she gulped it down. 'Phfft! Gets you right in the gut!'

'Fark it,' said Ludor. Something gut-wrenching could be just the thing to see the job through, and only losers said no to a premium Leffel elixir. As the squad cheered him on, he drank a jug without taking a breath then winced. 'It's barely better than brew.' He grunted in disappointment.

'I thought you appreciated the finer things in life, but there's just no pleasing you, is there?'

'I've had far better.' It didn't even come close to matching the elixir he'd had with Boss King on numerous occasions.

'You is posh then, aye?' said SHARP, nudging BRISK with a grin.

Perhaps to prove to the squad, he kept drinking and caught up to them in no time. Debrov downed one after another, proving something to her commander that she didn't quite understand.

FIERCE was the first to fall. She bent forward with a groan, then smacked the floor face-first. Debrov made some comment about her not able to hold her elixir before keeling over in pain. She sniffed her mug then glowered at Gelda while attempting to scream obscenities that came out as groans. She hurled her mug into a wall where it smashed. She lunged at Gelda but collapsed halfway there. FORCE puked, BRISK gasped for air, then they both collapsed. SHARP backed towards the wall but didn't make it, while FIERCE coughed up blood and blacked out, followed by FORCE, Debrov, then the others.

Ludor looked to Gelda who had finished dressing wounds and wiping blood, and now made her friends comfortable with cushions from the broken chairs and towels from the bathroom.

'Poison?' Ludor inquired.

'Soured elixir laced with pest repellent.' As she put a second cushion behind Prinn's head, Gelda's blank expression revealed neither pride nor shame.

With a grunt, Ludor tossed the jug aside. Why couldn't a job just go to plan for once? He slapped his squad around, kicking them for added measure. None moved; they barely breathed. It seemed they were also heading to medical, which meant he was down a squad. Of all the inconveniences! Suddenly he felt too tired to move. Assuming it was the elixir, he waited for fate to deal its blow, but he didn't fall or pass out. He'd had this feeling before. It was nothing to do with the elixir and everything to do with his general disenchantment. *Fark!*

Gelda pick up a piece of broken toy. Dust trickled out. A metallic scent filled her nostrils.

Ludor blindly watched her try to arrange unrecognisable pieces of the irrevocably damaged biospheres back together and got the feeling she was as lost as he was. Feeling an affinity with a Leffel brought back his lost rage. 'Why am I still standing?'

Gelda looked at him too closely and shrugged. 'I guess you're not a pest.'

'What?' He had no idea what she meant.

As their eyes locked, Ludor felt vulnerable under her gaze, as if she could see his thoughts.

Gelda slumped to the floor and sighed. With a slow shake of her head, she spoke quietly. 'Do you have any clue what you've just done? You destroyed five biospheres!'

'I didn't. *They* did!' He instantly regretted the objection. What the fark was wrong with him, and why did he feel bad but not in a good way? *Fark!*

'Each was a unique and complete system of living organisms, meticulously grown and nurtured. They were *alive*.' Gelda slowly approached him. 'Squillions of lives are now gone forever so a man with no appreciation for a living miracle can admire a severed one. What an absolute shameful and unnecessary disaster.'

To appease the guilt that he didn't understand, Ludor stormed towards Gelda and yanked the pack off her back. He shook out the contents.

'I don't have it. And you can put to sleep whatever diabolical Plan B you're devising, because you're too late. It's already built, which means it's too late to sever it.'

Ludor's heightened sense for deception had served him well over the centuries. It was to blame for most of his notorieties, but Gelda's statement confused him. His trained ears knew an untruth when they heard one, and yet Leffels didn't lie. The conflict brought him to a crossroad.

Possible events played out in his mind. Regardless of lies and deceptions, telling Boss King the toy was built might work in his favour. Or he could vanish without a trace. There were no Gorgons here to witness it. He could leave proof with Debrov that the toy was built so she could report to Boss King when she recovered from the poisoning. That would neatly cancel the job. How Debrov would explain his disappearance was an issue. Her precarious nature was ridiculously unpredictable. No, vanishing was taking a big chance with his freedom. Constantly looking over his shoulders with the persistent threat of a head-jarring looming would stifle his freedom. He couldn't risk that. The release pass annulled his agreement with the Empire, fair and square. It was his best bet. The only way forward was to trust his instincts.

Ludor rubbed his face with rough hands. Fark! Give me a

break – one break – that's all I ask!

A glare aimed at Gelda went unseen as she focussed on something on the floor near the unconscious Leffels. Had she not thrown him a look of panic before rushing for it, he might've missed his chance. He was closer and got there first.

With a smile, Ludor picked up a handheld disc with a large button in its centre that read *Closed*. Holding it to his ear, tapping and shaking it, and brushing a hand over it didn't reveal its purpose.

'What is this?!'

'The spactor,' said Gelda, amused that the word meant nothing to him.

'What the fark is a spactor?' He turned it over and saw a latch that he slid open to see coordinates flashing on a map of Leffon. It was some kind of travel device! A moment of impulsive decision-making kicked in fast. He studied the data on its tiny screen then tossed it with great force towards the window. It smashed through the glass and sailed through. He had to stop Mutt from chasing it.

'No!' Gelda cried.

Ludor expected her to go after it, and she almost did, but she was more interested in what he would do next. *Watch and learn,* he thought. He swivelled the chain around the hound's neck to locate the Anon ball, then entered the coordinates from the spactor. He let Mutt have a sniff.

'Woof!'

Destination confirmed, Ludor went to the foyer door and slapped his thigh. 'Come!' he called to Mutt in a gruff though gentle tone. From his position, lying halfway between them to one side, Mutt's ears pricked.

'Come here, boy!' Gelda countered. Mutt's head raised and turned to her.

'Here, Mutt!' Ludor encouraged. 'That's a good boy!' Tail wagging, Mutt got up and sauntered towards him.

Gelda clapped her hands. 'Over here, Mutt!' Mutt stopped and turned.

Simultaneously, they enticed the hound.

'Come here, beautiful boy!'

'You wanna play?'

'Who's a sweet boy? You're a sweet boy!'

Roused into a frenzy, Mutt wiggled and turned in circles with his tail whipping at his head, ears flailing, tongue lolling, and mouth widening as the transformation from hound to portal began. With every opposing command, Mutt turned his smearing head from side to side. Eyes and facial fur disappeared, and his mouth dominated, swirling into a vortex of shadow and light. He took a few steps towards Gelda, then to Ludor and back again, scampering up and down the room, unable to settle on his loyalties. When he finally made his choice, other than the hint of a tail at the end of a spiralling maelstrom, he was mostly a portal.

'Good boy!' Ludor praised as Mutt opened his portal mouth wide.

Gelda approached and said quietly, 'Don't give it to him.'

It took Ludor a moment to realise what she meant. He groaned. 'For farksake, it's just a toy! It's over. Go find another hobby!'

'It's *not* a toy!' What would it take for him to understand?! 'Are you deliberately refusing to recognise it as a living entity?'

With a foot poised at the threshold, Ludor thought about replying, but had nothing, not even a quip, though there was a certain heaviness to the task ahead and a sense that it wouldn't achieve much. In all likelihood, he wasn't getting his release pass from Boss King – not the honest way at least. It would be from violence as usual, but what choice did he have? Leffels were good at thinking and conceiving. While it was a fine challenge to match their prowess with his own brand of wiliness, this wasn't the time for consideration. Sticking to the task was all he had and indulging a Leffel's mind tricks wasn't going to get him what he wanted.

'All those squillions of lives lost for a collection,' Gelda continued while he stupidly stood there instead of leaving. 'And then what – more obsessions? There are more worthwhile pursuits than stealing cherished possessions and ending lives. Taking from others for your own gain never ends well. Make your own choices, Commander. What do *you* want to do?' Gelda got so close he saw bright speckles in her eyes. 'What are *you* getting out of this?'

With a shake of his head, he turned long enough to blurt, 'Freedom!' While it was good to say it out loud, he seethed that she'd extracted his secret. If he wasn't so farking lost and confused, he'd shut her up by knocking her out. With one final smouldering scowl, he lowered a foot inside the bioportal and onto Mutt's tongue which had already turned into a slippery moving walkway. Ahead, the vortex swirled faster while his mind went to tactics. *Another Leffon world, more Leffels. Be ruthless and forceful, do whatever it takes to get the toy and get out.* A second foot down made him realise that he'd drastically underestimated the enemy when a much-too-familiar stench of decay filled his nostrils. *Trongarl?*

The Leffel had tricked him!

His only hope was to abort the trip, which meant turning back around, but the thickened slobber made him slip and fall. Groping about, he grabbed at gooey flesh, but his hands went right through, as it had almost fully transitioned into compacted space. As the tongue walkway carried him forward, he felt the release pass slipping from his grasp.

A new fear surfaced. When Mutt delivered him to Dirt City without the toy, he would lose everything earned over ten centuries – admiration, influence, and status. Before now, they were worthless, but compared to the future that awaited him, they were a fortune. He would lose this life and many more to come and almost certainly spend his immediate future head-jarred. *Fark!*

Without hesitation, Gelda went after Ludor only to get pulled back. She turned to find Alrick holding her arm.

'You can't go after him!' he said.

She writhed free. 'If I don't, he'll get the Universe!'

Arms across chest, Alrick shook his head. 'He won't. I scrambled the spactor coordinates. He thinks he's going to Anon, but it's taking him back to Dirt City.'

It took a moment for Gelda to figure out what he meant then she frowned. 'How long were you conscious for?'

'I woke while you were dressing wounds and the Gorgons were drinking.'

'What exactly did you do to the dog?'

Alrick chuckled. 'I reset its coordinates to Trongarl. It was the only thing I could think to do.'

'You tricked the commander?'

'I suppose I did, but you poisoned the trievers and lied.'

'I did.'

They laughed.

'Are we becoming Gorgons?'

'Only to outwit them.'

The bioportal wavered and faded until there was nothing left except the lingering smell of wet dog. Gelda insisted Alrick keep an eye on the unconscious Leffels while she bolted out the door to reclaim the spactor. She found it in a puddle below the window. It was wet and chipped, but when she wiped it down and switched it on, the large button turned green and read, *Open*. Absently strapping it to her waist, she returned to the clubhouse and joined Alrick who sat back against an erect portion of wall so they could talk.

Gelda took a good look around and couldn't fathom the mindless destruction of people and property. The Domers had lost their lives and their games, there were poisoned Gorgons unconscious on the floor, and the clubhouse was in tatters.

'We fought hard to protect our games,' Alrick said quietly, his eyes on their friends. 'They lost their lives for them.'

'They'll rebirth,' Gelda assured him. While true, it didn't make it any easier to accept. 'Perhaps their next lives will be better. Given time, they might even decide to get new Cosmo Domes.'

Alrick held up the device he'd been tampering with since Gelda left for Anon. 'They may not need to get new ones. I have biodata from an earlier save point.'

'Meaning?'

'Meaning our biospheres may not be completely lost.'

Gelda's eyes went from wearily gazing into nowhere to being entirely focussed on Alrick. 'They're safe?'

'In theory. They need preservation chambers though. Hopefully Tolbert has some suggestions.'

'A small chance is better than none.' Gelda got up and stretched. While exhausted, her bones didn't ache, and nothing was hurting. Even her mind was clear. She felt better than she had in centuries. 'Let's look forward. There is always hope, although I'm concerned that commander will be back when he figures out we duped him.'

'Renoy said that when high ranking Gorgons fark up, they get head-jarred, so I doubt we'll see him again.'

'I'm not even going to ask what that means,' said Gelda with a shiver.

They caught each other up on what led them to the moment. As Gelda finished telling him about the Universe progress, sirens sounded in the street below. Flashing red lights lit up the windows that weren't smashed.

Alrick held up the wrist that had his aide strapped to it. 'I put through peacekeeper and nurse requests. You get back to Anon to finish building your Universe. I'll stay here.'

'I'm not leaving you to deal with this mess alone!'

'There's nothing you can do here. The peacekeepers will send the Gorgons home and the nurses will take care of our friends. When everyone has recovered and the Universe is built, we'll get together again.'

Down in the street, car doors slammed, and voices echoed up through the broken windows. The clink of the metal handrails announced the peacekeepers would soon arrive through the broken door of the club.

'This way is open,' the spactor said on repeat between two long pauses filled with bleeps. It bleeped and *Open* flashed on the button.

'Go and finish your Universe, Gelda!'

She pressed the button. The spactor rings came into full focus and a smell of mountain air wafted through. 'Message me the moment you have news,' she told Alrick. 'Tawawa!'

'Tawawa!' he replied with a wave.

With a smile, Gelda stepped through the fully charged rings back to Anon to save her beloved Universe.

Not The End!

Thanks for reading!

If you enjoyed *A Faulty Universe Begins*, please
leave a review on your favourite book site.
As an independent author I depend on (and appreciate)
your support to continue writing.

If you haven't already, head to my website at
www.tayawood.com and sign up to my mailing list.
It's your best source of news about future releases,
including the next book in the *Cosmo Dome* series:
A Glitchy Galaxy Gets a GOD.

About The Author
TAYA WOOD

With a career as a graphic designer and communications specialist behind her, Taya now writes fantastical stories. Passionate about speculative fiction from an early age, favourite authors include Martha Wells, V.E. Schwab, Becky Chambers, Philip Pullman, Holly Black, Ben Elton, and Charles de Lint. Taya writes from an off-grid tiny homestead in a forest on the Sunshine Coast, Queensland where she lives with her husband who's a theme park designer, and a fluffy grey cat for a muse. When she's not pondering absurdities, Taya enjoys improv dance, freestyle frisbee, and exploring the natural world, often all at once.

WWW.TAYAWOOD.COM

Acknowledgements

I wrote this book in secret and solitude, but massive thanks go to three key people who brought it to life. Danita for the tools and guidance to build it, Tracey whose insightful observations steered a crucial scene development, and Mark for too many conversations to count that helped to conceive, develop, and troubleshoot. Thanks also go to family and friends for support and encouragement once the secret was out, particularly Natasha and Faith-Marie.

Glossary

PLACES

Oridian: A higher realm of existence and home to worlds of all shapes and sizes inhabited by immortal people.

Leffon: A territory of twelve utopian worlds in the higher realm of Oridian.

Equion: A sunny Leffon world.

Anon: An isolated Leffon world.

Gorgonia: a territory of dystopian worlds in the higher realm of Oridian.

Trongarl: a Gorgonia world dominated by the Madrik Empire.

PEOPLE

Leffels: happy, optimistic immortal people who live pleasant lives doing what they love and being kind and considerate.

Gorgons: disagreeable and aggressive immortal people who enjoy brawling, ruining things, and finding ways to make things worse.

COSMO DOME GAMING SYSTEM

Cosmo Dome: the connected and activated preservation chamber and powerstation.

Preservation Chamber: the self-contained space in which a cosmo dome biosphere exists and functions.

Powerstation: The source of power for a cosmo dome biosphere.

Mainframe: processes, analyses, and converts information, and connects the system to workstations and peripherals.

Controller: provides input to the cosmo dome system, and controls objects and avatars in the game.